Georgie

CHOICES

BILL MYERS

TRUTH SEEKERS

CHOICES

B&H KIDS

Nashville, Tennessee

978-1-4336-9081-5

Published by B&H Publishing Group,
Nashville, Tennessee

Dewey Decimal Classification: JF
Subject Heading: ADVENTURE FICTION \
TRUTH—FICTION \ MACHINERY—FICTION

Literary agent for Author is Alive Communications,
Inc., 7680 Goddard Street, Colorado Springs, Colorado,
80920, www.alivecommunications.com.

1 2 3 4 5 6 7 8 • 18 17 16 15 14

For Terry Mendel . . .

Prayer warrior extraordinaire

Choose for yourselves this day whom you will serve.

—JOSHUA 24:15 NIV

Chapter One

BEGINNINGS . . .
ALL OVER AGAIN

J
A
K
E

"Dad!" I shouted.

Look, I don't want to complain (that specialty belongs to Jenny, my twin sister) but seriously, snoring camels?

"Gita!"

Sleeping in my tent!

"Robbie!"

It's not that I don't love animals. I've always taken great care of pets . . . well, except the time Jenny went to camp and asked me to look after her goldfish, Bob. Hey, it wasn't my fault he ate the whole box of fish food I'd tossed in. (He should have been called a *pig*fish.) And you really can't blame me that Fred, her cat, tried scooping Bob's dead body off the water, knocking the fish bowl on top of her dog, named Dog. (Jenny can be a little challenged in the naming department.) And how was I to know Dog would chase Fred into the street and lose at playing tag with a semitruck to become little Doggy and Freddy Frisbees? (May they all rest in peace.)

But snoring camels in my tent? Not cool.

Still, they were better than the two rats I suddenly noticed sleeping on my pillow.

"Isaac!"

But, of course, nobody came to my rescue because everybody was fighting off their own animals . . . which is just the sort of thing to happen when you're in the Israeli desert with an experimental Machine that has created a super holographic image of Noah's ark that's so real every person (and animal) thinks it is real.

Confused?

Welcome to my world. Unfortunately, it gets worse.

I threw off the covers, slipped on a T-shirt that didn't smell too bad, and staggered out of my tent. Actually, I share the tent with Robbie, Dad's crazy inventor. But Robbie was in jail after his time beam generator accidentally turned him into a teenager.

Hey, I told you it gets worse.

After stumbling over a couple of giant tortoises, I made it out of the tent only to see lions and tigers and pears. (Sorry, the bears weren't around, but if it helps two monkeys were munching on that fruit.)

I squinted against the morning sun and shouted to

Jenny, who was just stepping out of her tent. "What's going on?"

"We're still being invaded by animals."

"You think?" I pushed aside a baby crocodile approaching my bare foot and eyeing my tootsies. "What are these types of critters doing out here in the desert?"

"They have escaped from the Jerusalem zoo," Gita, Jenny's tent mate, said. You'd like Gita. She's from India or someplace like that, and out of the twenty or so workers Dad has at this archeological site, she and Robbie are the brightest. She continued, "Like all of the other animals, they have sensed the ark's presence."

I looked across the tents to the Machine—a giant flat area with a hundred tall poles all around it. Ibrahim (an Arab guy complete with robe and cool headdress) and Isaac (a muscular Jewish guy complete with one of those little beanie things on his head) had built a makeshift fence around the Machine last night. It was the only way to keep the animals from squeezing into it and crushing each other. And for good reason. Because there, sitting smack dab in its center, was a giant projected image of Noah's ark—with Noah and his family working away. Everything about them was so real, it fooled you into thinking it was real (you and every pair of animals on the planet).

"Gita, we gotta do something!" I yelled. "Can't you figure out how to fix the Machi—Oh crud!" The "Can't you figure out" part was to Gita. The "Oh, crud!" was to the pile of elephant manure my foot just stepped in. Actually, it was my foot, my ankle, and half of my shin (they were pretty big elephants).

Gita called back, "Robbie is the only individual who can repair the Machine."

Hazel, another one of those genius types, but with clothes that looked like she shopped at Ringling Brothers Circus and a personality so cheery you just want to slap her, chimed in. "Maybe we should try breaking him out of jail again." She was riding one of the elephant fertilizer plants alongside Maximilian, her gum-chewing chimpanzee.

"Well, somebody's gotta do something!" I repeated.

"I fully agree," Gita called back. "However, you may first wish to reevaluate your priorities."

"What's that?" I asked. I noticed that she, Jenny, and Hazel were all staring at the same thing . . . which explains why they all yelled at the same time:

"RUN!"

I looked over my shoulder. They had a good point. Actually, two good points . . . and they belonged to the horns of the giant Brahman bull charging straight at me.

Normally, I would have turned and coolly strolled away, since cool is one thing I know how to be. But since dead is one thing I don't want to be, I turned, calmly threw my hands into the air, and ran off screaming like a little girl.

It was a pretty good plan and would have worked, if it weren't for that sleeping rhinoceros. Well, he had been sleeping, until I tripped and fell onto his giant head . . . which he threw up in the air . . . which flew me up in the air . . . which meant calmly throwing my hands up in the air, and once again screaming like a little girl. (Practice makes perfect.)

The good news is, what goes up

!

H

H

H

G

U

A

must come

A

U

G

H

H

H

!

down.

The bad news is, down can sometimes be a little pain-ful—especially if it's onto the top of one of our giant

THUD!

transport trucks.

Luckily, there was no pain. (It's hard to feel pain when you've been knocked unconscious.)

Unluckily, that was about as lucky as things would get for a while.

Chapter Two

A NOT-SO-GREAT ESCAPE

J
E
N
N
I
F
E
R

"But why do *I* have to go?" I argued.

"I need someone to sneak in the time beam generator," Dad said, "and they'd never suspect a little girl."

"I'm almost fourteen!"

"Exactly."

"What about Isaac? Why can't he go with you? Or Hazel or Ibrahim?"

"They've already been there. The police would recognize them and throw them in jail alongside Robbie. You, on the other hand, you're just a cute—"

"Little girl," I said in my best sarcasm.

"Precisely." (Sometimes Dad doesn't get sarcasm.)

I gave a drama-queen sigh and threw in my best eye roll, which he totally didn't get, either.

I definitely was not crazy about sneaking into jails and helping people escape—especially if it meant getting caught and serving twenty years to life. But since the rest of Dad's archeological team hadn't returned from their mini-vacation, and since Jake was still milking his *I-almost-died* concussion, that left Gita and me. And since Gita was in charge of the site whenever Dad was away, that meant no amount of sarcasm or eye rolling would do the trick.

So two and a half hours later, Dad and I were riding up some ancient elevator to the third-floor jail cells. I know I wanted some quality father–daughter time, but this was ridiculous. It was even more ridiculous the way the rickety old elevator swayed and jerked like a crazy amusement park ride. But finally, after more than a couple prayers from yours truly, the doors rattled open. And there behind a desk sat the same redheaded receptionist Hazel had sent back in time just a few days ago. Behind her was a locked door to the hallway that led to the cells.

"May I help you?" she asked.

"Yes," Dad cleared his throat. "We've come to visit Dr. Robert P. Ruttledge."

The look on her face said his name definitely brought back some bad memories. "Visiting hours are over for the morning," she snapped. "Come back after lunch."

"I'm afraid you don't understand," Dad said. "This is an emergency."

"And I'm afraid you didn't hear me. Come back after lunch or don't come back at all!" (They must have been some real bad memories.)

Dad gave me a nod and I reached into my coat pocket for the time beam generator. It was about the size of a large flashlight.

"I was hoping it wouldn't come to this," he said.

The woman reached for her phone. "And I'm hoping you'll stay right here so security can throw you out."

"Now, Jen," Dad said.

I pulled out the generator and turned it on. It began its usual **HUMMM**-ing as the little multicolored lenses in front began their usual spinning.

The receptionist looked at it and sighed, "Oh no, not again."

"I'm sorry," Dad said. He gave me another nod. I pointed the generator at her, pulled the trigger and

FLASH

she was gone—disappeared from sight.

"Good girl," Dad said. "What did you set it on?"

"6:15 this morning."

"Excellent. She'll arrive in her bed and think this was all just a dream." He reached for her desk phone and fiddled with the buttons until the lock on the door to the hallway buzzed open. Unfortunately, his sausage fingers also managed to hit the alarm button and the red light above the door suddenly began to flash.

"Oops," he said.

"Nice move," I said.

"Thanks," he said. (I told you he's no good at sarcasm.)
"We better get going!"

He threw open the hallway, door, and we raced down
a long corridor with jail cells on each side. But they didn't
have bars. Instead, each cell had a locked steel door with
a thick little window. We checked each window until we
spotted Robbie. Only it wasn't the Robbie I remembered.
Instead of some weirdly dressed guy in his late twenties
wearing a Mexican sombrero, Hawaiian shirt, and sandals,
this Robbie was some weirdly dressed sixteen-year-old
whose face looked like the before in one of those before-
and-after acne ads.

"Reduce power to fifty percent," Dad said.

I flipped a little switch on the side of the generator.
According to Hazel this would give us enough power to
move the person through time but not through space.

"Adjust the future date to AD 2122."

"2122?" I cried. "That'll make him way over a hundred
years old!"

"It's only temporary. And it's the only way to get him
out. Hurry!"

Normally, I would have argued (or at least thrown in
another good eye roll), but Dad looked like he knew what
he was talking about so I turned the date to AD 2122.

Dad tapped on the little window to get Robbie's attention. And when the boy looked up, Dad shouted, "Fire!"

I pulled the trigger and

FLASH

sure enough, once the light faded, there was Robbie—only now he was an old Robbie. Real old. Fossil old. So old he was grabbing his chest and dropping to his knees.

"What's wrong?" I yelled.

"Heart attack."

"He's so old, he's dying of a heart attack!"

"It's all part of the plan."

"What are you talking about?"

Before he could answer, the hallway door flew open and two security guards ran in with rifles raised. "Throw down your weapons!" the tallest one shouted.

"We have no weapons," Dad shouted back. "But you're just in time. One of your prisoners is having a heart attack."

"What?"

Dad pointed through the window. "See for yourself."

As they ran toward us, I quietly slipped the time beam generator back into my coat pocket.

"Move!" they shouted. "Step away from the window!"

We obeyed and they arrived, pressing against the window for a look. Seeing the problem, the shorter guard fumbled with a bunch of keys on his belt until he found the right one and slid it into the lock. Dad and I traded looks as they opened the door and stepped in to help Robbie.

"Give me the generator," Dad whispered.

I slipped it to him.

Without a word, he turned the power back up to one hundred percent, adjusted the date to twenty minutes into the past. Then he pointed it at the two men, and

FLASH

they were gone. Well not gone, gone. More like gone to wherever they were twenty minutes ago.

Meanwhile, Robbie was on the floor, still holding his chest and doing a pretty good job of dying. Dad raced into the cell, readjusted the power to fifty percent and reset the date to: *CURRENT.*

He fired and

FLASH

The light faded and there was the Robbie I'd always known (and tried to like), complete with his long braided hair and childish humor.

"You're back!" I shouted.

"And my front." He motioned to his chest and stomach. (See what I mean about childish?)

Helping him to his feet, Dad said, "The alarm is still flashing; we haven't much time."

We raced out of the cell and down the hall into the reception area. After hitting the elevator button one, two . . . a hundred times, the doors finally rattled open and the three of us piled in.

After pressing the button one, two . . . two hundred times, the doors finally rattled closed and we headed down to the lobby. For whatever reason, it was a lot slower going down than going up and a *whole lot* bumpier.

"W-w-what's wrong with this th-th-thing?" I shouted (which is exactly how you shout when you're getting knocked around like a ping pong ball). "It wasn't like thi-thi-this going up!"

"It's th-th-the extra weight!" Robbie shouted.

"Wh-wh-what?" Dad yelled.

"There's to-to-too many of us! We have to-to-to—"
Before he could finish there was a loud

SNAP

above our heads. The whole elevator lunged to the left and
threw us into the wall.

"Wh-wh-what happened?" I yelled

"One of the cables snapped!" Dad shouted.

"Too m-m-much weight!" Robbie repeated.

"What do we do?" I cried.

"Here," Robbie grabbed the time beam generator from
Dad, "let me have that." He aimed it at Dad. It began to
HUMMM as the lenses began to spin.

"Are yo-yo-you crazy?" Dad shouted.

"No m-m-more than usual!" Robbie adjusted the generator's dials on the side. "I'm sending you to the c-c-camp
this morning s-s-so we have less weight."

"Robbie!" Dad cried.

"It's c-c-cool!" Robbie shouted. By now the little lenses
in front had begun twirling full speed. "Catch you later,
dude-ude-ude!" he yelled as he pulled the trigger. But, just
as he pulled it, the elevator gave another violent jerk, this
time throwing us into the right wall. Still, Robbie managed
to fire the

FLASH

generator. As the light faded, we saw Dad had disappeared.
And, now that we'd lost the extra weight, the shaking
stopped. There was, however, one little problem . . .

"Uh-oh," Robbie said.

"Uh-oh what?" I asked.

He motioned to the side of the generator and I looked. The dial was no longer set for this morning. It was set for:

"1961?" I cried.

"It must have changed when we slammed into the wall."

"You sent my father back to 1961?"

"Don't panic, you're reading it upside down." He flipped the generator around. "See, if you read it this way it says—"

"1961!" I repeated.

"Hmm . . ." He turned it back and forth. "Will you look at that."

"You sent my father back to 1961?"

He didn't answer but kept turning the generator around and around, impressed that the date always read the same. (Sometimes genius types get a little sidetracked.)

And, if that wasn't bad enough . . . remember I said there was one little problem? I lied. There were two.

The second came when the elevator doors opened and there before us stood one gazillion guards, none of them looking real happy, and all of them pointing their weapons.

Chapter Three

A SURPRISE VISIT

J
E
N
N
I
F
E
R

Of course we were majorly worried about Dad and we wanted to go get him, but we had a minor little problem of being arrested and thrown into an interrogation room.

Still, all good things must come to an end. Two hours later—or three or four (time drags when you're about to be tortured to death)—the door to our tiny cubicle opened and in walked our third or fourth interrogator. (Interrogators blur when they're about to torture you to death.) The man was big, bald, and looked grumpier than the other two . . . or three. He pulled a chair out from the table, turned it around and sat down. "So," he said, "I trust you find our accommodations comfortable?" He tried to smile, but it came out more like a sneer. Still, I appreciated the effort. (If a guy's going to torture you to death, he should at least be polite about it.)

But Robbie wasn't so polite. Not only did he refuse to comment on our accommodations (like the lack of cable TV, room service, or the lack of a room), he got right to the point. "How much longer are you going to hold us here?"

"It all depends," the big man said.

"On what?"

"On how much longer you're going to lie to us."

"We've been telling you the truth," Robbie said. "The dude stole our company's microchip and I was trying to catch him."

The man looked down at the chart in his hands. "By flying a rocket-powered gyrocopter directly into his Jeep."

"That was an accident."

The man scoffed.

"It's true."

"He says you're lying."

"He's lying."

The big fellow shook his head in disbelief just like the other two . . . or three. Finally, he turned to me. "And you insist on agreeing with him, that all his lies are true?"

My mouth was bone dry. "Yes," I croaked, then frowned and shook my head. "I mean, no."

"Pardon me?"

"Yes, I agree with his lies. I mean, no, they're not lies. I mean yes, I agree with them since they're not lies, which makes them the truth which means I—"

"Silence!"

It sounded like a pretty good idea. I nodded and gratefully sat back in my chair.

It was Robbie's turn. "What she's saying is that I'm telling the truth. And she should know. She was in the Jeep with the driver."

The man turned to me. "Is that true?"

I nodded, this time deciding to keep my mouth shut.

He sighed and rolled his head from side to side. It snapped and crackled like a bowl of Rice Krispies. Rising from his chair, he said, "And that is your final answer?"

We both nodded and swallowed. Well, Robbie swallowed; it was harder for me since my mouth was still as dry as a sand dune microwaved on high for thirty minutes, then baked at 450 degrees, and thrown into a clothes dryer.

TRANSLATION: My mouth was a little dry.

The big man was definitely not happy as he turned and started for the door.

"Where you going?" Robbie asked.

"We have a witness."

Robbie and I traded looks.

"A third party," he said. Then turning back to us one last time, he added, "You are certain you do not wish to change your story?"

We both nodded.

"All right then." He reached for the door, opened it, and called down the hall, "Send in the witness."

We waited. Again I tried to swallow and again I failed. A moment later, in walked . . .

"Jesse!" I gasped.

He looked at me and grinned that killer grin of his. Even though I was so mad I could spit (if I had anything to spit), I felt my stomach do those little flip-flops that happen whenever he's around.

"Are these the two you spoke of?" the man asked.

Jesse nodded, "Yes, sir."

The interrogator sighed, gave his neck another work out, then looked at us. "Okay, you are free to go."

"What?" Robbie asked. "Just like that?"

"Your stories match. The kid collaborated all of your facts."

Our jaws dropped.

The man turned, strolled out the door, and headed down the hall. But not before apologizing for all the misery he'd put us through for the last several hours.

Well, at least it was his version of an apology: "Have a nice day."

• • • • • • • •

Then there was Jesse's version. "Look, I'm sorry, okay?" he said as we walked towards Dad's pickup in the police station parking lot. "How many times do I have to apologize?"

That was only apology number four. I figured he had a couple hundred more to go.

"Well, at least you returned the microchip," Robbie

said. "Without it we couldn't have gotten the Machine up and running."

"And don't forget, I hid it from my mom's team so they couldn't use it."

Jesse's mom was also an archeologist. She had a site just a few miles away from Dad's and was working on an invention similar to the Machine. It's true, he did help some guy steal our microchip for her, but it's also true he changed his mind and returned it.

But that didn't mean I had to talk to him—at least, yet. And it certainly didn't mean I was going to look at him. No sir. One glance into those incredible blue eyes and I'd be a goner.

"Alrightee," Robbie said as he climbed behind the wheel of the pickup. "Let's get back to camp and bring your pop home." We joined him as he adjusted his seat then held out his hand to me. "Keys please?"

I turned to him.

"You don't have the keys?" he said.

"They're with Dad."

Robbie shook his head. "Not cool, dudette, not cool."

"Where's your Dad?" Jesse asked.

"1961."

"*What?*" He leaned forward and looked at us, obviously not appreciating the finer details of time travel.

Neither of us bothered to answer.

"Well," Robbie sighed. "I guess we'll go get him."

I nodded, reached into my pocket, and pulled out the time generator the police had given back to me.

"I'm sorry," Jesse said, staring at it. "How's a weird looking flashlight going to get your dad?"

Like I said, he didn't exactly understand the finer details. He understood them less when I turned on the generator

HUMMM

and the multicolored lenses in front began to twirl.

"Jen . . ." He sounded a little nervous.

I turned to Robbie and said, "So which one of us is going?"

"If we're doing this, we're all going to need to go."

I nodded.

"Doing what?" Jesse asked. "All going where?" He sounded a little more nervous.

"1961," I said. I turned the time beam generator around and aimed it at us.

"Wait a minute!" He sounded *a lot* nervous.

"Make sure you shoot all three of us," Robbie said.

"*Shoot!*" Jesse cried.

"It's no big deal," I said. "We're just going back to 1961 to get my dad." I reached for the trigger and started to pull.

"1961!" he yelled. "I wasn't even alive in 19—"

"Hold it!" Robbie shouted.

I turned to him.

"The dude's got a point."

I frowned.

"None of us were alive in 1961."

"So?"

"So, if you send us back in time before we're alive . . ."

I pulled my finger from the trigger and finished his thought. "Then we won't be alive?"

"Bingo." Ever so gently, he pushed aside the generator so it wasn't aimed at us.

"So how are we going to get him?" I asked.

Robbie frowned. "I'm not sure . . . not yet."

"You're not sure? We sent Dad all that way into the past, and you don't know how to bring him back?" My voice started to tremble. "Are you saying we lost him forever?"

He shook his head. "Not forever. You'll see him again when he catches up to us."

"And when is that?"

He did a quick calculation and answered, "Just over fifty years."

Chapter Four

JUST DROPPING IN

J
A
K
E

"You be careful up there!" Isaac called to me.

"No prob," I shouted back.

"I'm serious, one concussion per day is enough."

"Relax, I do this all the time."

"Really?" he said. "They have a lot of top-secret super holographic image projectors in Malibu, do they?"

Of course he was talking about the Machine's 1,085 giant projectors displaying the image of Noah and the ark down onto the staging area. The 1,085 projectors mounted onto the 110 poles surrounding that area. And he was right, there aren't too many of them back home. But since I am kinda like an expert at anything athletic (as long as it doesn't involve pain or working up a sweat), climbing the poles and adjusting the projectors was a piece of cake—especially if it meant staying high above all those thousands of animals—particularly the ones with long pointed horns and cranky dispositions.

And the view up there was pretty good too. Not only could I see Noah and his family sweating away building their boat, but I could check out the party scene some folks were having on the hill beside it. And you didn't have to be a nuclear scientist to tell who was having the most fun.

"Jake!" Isaac shouted.

I ignored him. My eyes had landed on a blonde chick that all the hilltop guys were teasing and harassing. And for good reason. She was just a few years older than me and über-gorgeous. She also had the most innocent and sensitive eyes I'd ever seen. It really bugged me the way the guys wouldn't leave her alone.

"Yo, Jake, you with us?"

I looked back to Isaac.

"The projector?" he said. "You're supposed to be working on the projector?"

"Right." I started looking for the plug. "I'm on it."

Earlier, at the control console a few dozen yards away, I'd asked Dad's team an important question. "Why don't you just shut the Machine down? You know, pull the plug?"

Gita had shaken her head. "Some of the animals entered the staging area before we erected the barrier. The images inside are so realistic that if we suddenly turn them off, it could harm the animal's limbic system."

I nodded like I knew what she was talking about.

The ever-cheery Hazel weighed in. "So we shut it down by slowly disengaging the projectors one at a time." She clapped her hands in excitement. "Oh, this will be such fun, fun, fun!"

Maximilian, her chimp, agreed, shouting, "Ooo-ooo, ahh-ahh, eee-eee." (Remember how I said sometimes you just wanted to slap Hazel for being so happy about everything? Well, it went double for monkey boy.)

"It is still very dangerous," Gita said, "and we may lose some animals. But at this juncture I see no alternative."

I didn't exactly agree with Hazel that this was fun since it didn't involve food or computer games or food or sleep or—did I mention food? But since I was light enough to climb the poles, I volunteered. (Who needs ladders when you got a great athlete like me around.) Besides, it was good to get above the swarming zoo below. Not only did it smell better, it was a whole lot safer.

The latest casualty had been over at the mess tent. Since none of the animals thought of packing a lunch for their little visit, and since none of the wooden cupboards in the giant tent had locks on them . . . well, let's just say it's hard to say no to a very hungry bear with very powerful claws. And once he turned those wooden cupboards into wooden splinters and dragged out all the food (making the mess tent a real mess), it was impossible to tell any of the other animals, no, either.

But it didn't stop there. Pretty soon anything in the camp that was edible, shredable, or poop-uponable was being eaten, shredded, or pooped upon. Even here at the

Machine. In fact, just a moment ago, the control console had become some hungry goat's between-meal snack.

"Get away!" Ibrahim shouted at him. "Shoo! Shoo!"

To which the goat turned, looked him squarely in the eye and

BURP-ed

Having made his point, the four-legged eating machine moved to another part of the panel with even more tasty capacitors, microchips and—

"NO, NOT THOSE WIRES!" Gita shouted. "They're alive with electricity. They'll—"

ZAP, CRACKLE, SIZZLE

. . . lots of smoke here, lots of smoke there

"Poor thing," Hazel said, running to the smoldering animal. He was alive but majorly shaken.

Isaac nodded. "Smoking is definitely hazardous to your health."

Needless to say, all the **ZAP**-ing, **CRACKL**-ing, and **SIZZL**-ing freaked out the other animals. They all began barking, howling, or growling—except for the butterflies who did a lot of -ing (because -ing is the sound butterflies make when they're freaked).

Unfortunately, some of the critters began to stampede this way and that, and that way and this. Unfortunatelier (is that a word?) this included Hazel's gum-chewing chimp. Unfortunateliest (maybe I should write my own dictionary) ape man thought the pole I was on would be the safest place, so he ran straight for it.

"No, Maximilian!" Hazel shouted. "No!" But of course it was impossible to hear her over all the howling, growling, and -ing.

"Get off!" I shouted. "Get down!" And even though that didn't sound a thing like *Come up here little fellow so your extra weight will snap off this pole and we'll both go crashing to the ground*, ape man ran right up the pole to join me.

It's not that I didn't enjoy his company. I just wasn't crazy about the way the pole started to

CREEEEEEEAK . . .

as it began to bend.

"Maximilian!" Hazel shouted. "Get down this instant!"

"She's right!" I shouted. "Listen to your master!"

But apparently banana breath had just found a new Best Friend Forever. So, instead of getting down, he crawled up my leg.

"Will you get down!"

Then up my chest.

"Get down!"

And my face.

"Miff mounnd! Miff mounnd!"

All this as the pole just kept

CREEEEEEEAK-ing . . .

until it finally led to the even more unpopular sound of it

BREAK-ing

in half and sending its two riders "Ahhhh-ing!" and "Ooo-ooo, ahh-ahh, eee-eee-ing" to the

THUD

ground.

Because ape man was a slightly better tree swinger than me, he managed to twist and turn so he landed outside the staging area.

I didn't.

The good news was my fall didn't hurt because it gave me another ticket into the land of Unconsciousville. The bad news was they'd moved Unconsciousville inside the staging area and onto Noah's ark.

Chapter Five

PREPARATIONS

J
E
N
N
I
F
E
R

"What do you mean, you'll go?" I said.

Jesse flipped the hair out of those incredible eyes. "I'm the reason your dad is back wherever he is. If I hadn't stolen that microchip, then Robbie wouldn't have tried to stop us and gotten arrested and—"

"—Dad wouldn't be back to 1961." I finished the sentence for him.

"Exactly."

I turned to Robbie, who was hunched over and working on the time beam generator in the Lab Tent. On the floor beside him sat a little glowing platform with pulsating lights all around it called the cross-dimensional folder. He'd worked out a pretty cool idea about connecting them so we could travel in time without getting older. "What do you think?" I asked him.

He answered without looking up. "About what?"

"Jesse going instead of me."

Still working, Robbie said, "Your boyfriend's got a point."

"He's not my—"

"But the dude's clueless what your pop looks like, especially back in 1961."

I was still thinking of the boyfriend crack and felt my ears getting hot the way they always do when I get embarrassed. Jesse saw my embarrassment (and probably felt his own) so he quickly changed subjects. "How old would your dad be back then?"

"I don't know," I said. "Five, six, maybe seven."

"You don't know when he was born?"

I glanced down, again embarrassed. A girl should probably know how old her own father is. Then again, with him gone all the time, we never really got that close. So whose fault is that? I bit my lip. I almost lost him last week and I had promised to think nicer thoughts. Usually, I did. But there were a whole lot of years of hurt to get over.

"You've seen pictures of him as a kid, right?" Jesse asked.

I frowned. "A couple." Then, brightening, I added, "And he'd be living with my grandma and I know what she looks like."

"When she was his young mother?" Robbie asked.

I slumped. He had me there.

"Don't sweat it," Robbie said.

"Why's that?" Jesse asked.

"'Cause neither of you are going. It's too dangerous."

"Too dangerous?" I said. "All you're doing is connecting the time beam generator with the dimensional folder. What's dangerous about that?"

"In my expert hands, nothing." (Robbie had obviously taken a few ego classes from my brother.) "But it's never been done before and I'm not experimenting with some kid."

I let the insult go. "You said all you had to do is connect the two machines and a person could travel any place in time without getting younger or older."

"True." He closed the panel on the side of the time beam generator. "With my incredible genius, it'll work perfectly. (See what I mean about ego?) But what's all this yick-yack about some shadow creature from a higher dimension?"

I swallowed. "Who told you that?"

"Queen Gita. She said it attacks you whenever we use the dimensional folder."

"I fought it off the last time."

"That's right," he smirked as he bent over the little dimensional folder platform on the floor. "Using a bunch of religious hocus-pocus, I hear."

"Beating back demons with the power of God is not hocus-pocus!"

Robbie looked up, surprised at my outburst. So did Jesse, though his look was more along the lines of, *What am I doing hanging out with this nut case of a girl?*

I pulled my hair behind my ears, which were suddenly hot again. Of course it was true. I had beaten back a demon with the power of God, at least that's what Gita said. But fighting demons isn't exactly the thing you say when trying to impress strangers . . . especially good looking ones with amazing blue eyes.

Robbie returned to his work, but Jesse kept staring, which, of course, meant my ears kept burning. After a century or two, he finally cleared his throat and asked, "Is that true? Did something like that really happen?"

I glanced down, fidgeting. "Long story."

He kept staring.

I kept fidgeting.

"Done." Robbie rose to his feet, wiping his hands. "As soon as Gita and the others retrieve your brother, I'll send one of the grown-ups back to search for your Pop and—"

"Dr. Robbie." His two-way communicator crackled to life with Gita's voice.

He pulled it from his pocket. "At your service, my lady."

She ignored him. "We are very much in need of you here at the staging area."

"No luck bringing Jud back?" he asked.

"That's Jake," I said.

He ignored me and listened as Gita spoke. "We cannot seem to locate him within the holograph image. Nor is he making any attempt to return to us from within it."

"Rodger-dodger, baby cakes. On my way."

"I, uh, um . . ." She sounded flustered.

He grinned. "The word you're looking for is thank you."

"Actually, those are two words," she said. "Now, if you wouldn't mind, please, hurry."

He slipped the communicator back into his pocket. "She likes me, I can tell." He turned and headed for the door. "You kiddies coming?"

"Give us a minute," I said.

"No problemo." Motioning back to the generator and dimensional folder, he added, "But don't be getting any lame ideas."

"Oh, we won't," I said with my sweetest smile.

He hesitated.

I cranked up my smile to Super Sweet.

"Dr. Robbie!" Gita's voice called. "Hurry!"

He gave me a final look of warning then, without a word, left the tent.

As soon as he was gone, I made a beeline for the time beam generator on the table.

"What are you doing?" Jesse asked. "He said nothing lame."

"There's nothing lame about a daughter trying to save her father. I picked up the generator, adjusted the dial to 1961 and flipped on the standby switch. As usual the little lenses on the front began spinning as the whole thing began to

HUMMM

I looked down to the dimensional folder on the floor.

The platform began glowing brighter and the little lights along the edge pulsated faster.

"Do you know what you're doing?" Jesse asked.

"Of course." It wasn't exactly a lie, but it wasn't exactly the truth, either. I crossed to the handheld computer Robbie used in connecting the generator and dimensional folder. There, on the tiny screen was the word:

LOCATION:

Under it was Dad's home address that Robbie had looked up earlier.

1233 MINNESOTA DRIVE

SEATTLE, WASHINGTON, USA

"Now what?" I asked, searching the keyboard.

Jesse approached and took a look. "Try hitting ENTER."

Okay, so I'm no computer geek. I reached over, hit ENTER and the lights down on the dimensional folder flashed faster. With the time beam generator still in my hand, I stepped onto the platform.

"Jenny?" he warned.

"Wish me luck," I said.

"You're not serious?"

"It's no big deal." I turned the generator around and pointed it at myself.

"No way!" Jesse reached for it but I blocked him. It was cute seeing him get all protective, but I knew what I was doing.

"I'll be right back," I said.

"I won't let you." He leaped onto the platform and lunged for the generator just as I pulled the trigger and fired.

The good news was the platform gave the old familiar

CRACKLE

followed by the always-blinding FLASH as I disappeared.

The bad news was, I wasn't the only one who had vanished.

Chapter Six

A DROP-IN GUEST

J
A
K
E

I woke up with an incredible ponding in my head . . . and itching all over my body. It took a second to figure out the itching came from the hay I was lying in. It took two seconds to realize it wasn't the hay but the fleas in the hay—the ones who were busy

chomp, chomp, chomp-ing

on me like I was their new main course.

And the pounding in my head?

It wasn't inside it, but beside it. *Real* beside . . . as in some guy wearing a dingy bathrobe hammering giant spikes into a wall two inches from my ear.

35

"HEY!" I cried (which is exactly the thing to cry when someone's trying to pierce your ear with a giant spike and hammer). I rolled away and staggered to my feet. But bathrobe boy didn't say a word; he just kept hammering.

"You might want to be more careful with that thing!" I yelled.

More hammering. More not saying a word.

"Hello?" I stepped closer and waved my hand in front of his face. "Yo, dude? Anyone home?"

He stopped, but just long enough to wipe the sweat off his face, grab another spike, and start hammering again. It was about this time I remembered I wasn't in Kansas any more. Or Israel. Or the twenty-first century. Well, I was, and I wasn't. I was inside the Machine's superholographic image. The one so real it fools all your senses into believing you're actually there . . . which of course you're not . . . which of course explains why you can feel the

chomp, chomp, chomp-ing

from all the make-believe fleas. It also explains why you can yell your lungs out at the projected image of some make-believe guy without ever being heard.

But, just to be sure, I tried one last time. "Nice robe," I shouted. "Leftover from the Christmas pageant?"

Nothing. No response to my insult (which was okay since he was still holding the giant hammer).

So . . . I was inside a holographic image of Noah's ark. Cool.

I leaned against one of the walls, watching the guy work. When I got tired of that, I leaned against another wall and watched. I don't want to be rude, but the excitement wasn't exactly killing me. Finally, I decided to do a little exploring.

I shoved my hands into my pockets, stepped out of the stall and moved to the second stall, which looked a lot like the first one. I strolled to the third, which looked a lot like the second, which looked a lot like the first. I strolled to the . . . Well, you get the picture. Granted, some were bigger, some smaller, but the interior decorator only had one style, Early American Barnyard. It was definitely not a five-star hotel. I couldn't even find the gift shop, let alone a pool. But wherever I went, there was no shortage of

chomp, chomp, chomp-ing.

And there was no shortage of hay (which would come in handy considering who the guests would be and the lack of bathroom facilities).

I eventually found a ladder and climbed up to the second deck. Same stalls, same hay, same fleas. I found another ladder and made my way up to the top deck. It was nearly dark, but the view was spectacular with mountains and meadows and forests. But there were no lakes or oceans or water of any kind (which can make building the world's first ocean liner a little embarrassing). However, there was something else.

Off in the distance, I saw what looked like a trail of animals heading my way. Closer still, on a nearby hill, I saw the lights I'd seen earlier. The laughter and music coming from it sounded like a good time was being had by all. Then, toward the front of the boat I heard what sounded like an argument. A couple guys were really going at it. Never being one to miss a good fight, I trotted toward it to see what was happening. And since Gita hadn't turned off the translation program, I understood everything perfectly.

I rounded the corner and there they were—some old guy, complete with white hair and a white beard, pacing back and forth talking to a younger guy.

"The sky, the clouds, they are heavy with rain. My son, you do not understand how soon God's judgment will come."

"You've been saying that all my life," the younger guy said.

"But it is true. By morning we will be finished. Ham, His promises will finally come to pass."

Ham, I snickered, *what a name.* Still, I figured it was better than Tuna or, worse yet, Chicken.

"And then what?" Ham asked. "This God of yours is supposed to flood the entire land. Father, there is not a single stream or river in sight. From where will this flood come?"

The old guy, who was obviously Noah, ran his hand through his beard. But before he answered, Ham continued.

"And the closer we come to finishing, the more the villagers laugh at us."

"They have always laughed at us. It is the price one must pay for obedience."

"And I've paid that price," Ham said. "Year after year."

Noah said nothing but turned to watch the setting sun.

Ham stepped closer. "The village is throwing a party."

Noah turned to him. "A party? Is that what they are calling it?"

It was Ham's turn to look away.

Nodding toward the lights, Noah said, "Have you seen what they do at these parties? The filth? The violence? Just speaking such things should make us blush."

"I am not saying I would join in. But . . . they are our friends, Father. Many of them my wife's family."

Noah remained silent.

Ham continued. "Do you have any idea what it is like to be cut off from your friends?"

"You have your family, here."

"I know, and we love you. But there's more." He nodded toward the lights. "So much more. Times change."

Noah stiffened. "God does not change. His ways are perfect. Nor does He lie. When He says He will judge the people for their great evil, He will judge the people."

"And our family is the only one He will save?"

"We are the ones who have chosen to obey and follow Him."

"Maybe we can talk others into obeying."

"We have tried. All of our lives you know we have tried. But their ears remain deaf." He shook his head. "No. God says we are the only ones to be saved."

"But maybe . . . maybe He is wrong. If we can talk others into coming on board and—"

"Ham. God is never wrong."

After a long pause, Ham finally answered. "I am going, Father. My wife and I, we will go to the party."

Noah looked back to the setting sun and said nothing.

"We shall return before sunrise."

"And if judgment should come tonight? While you are partying with your friends?"

"God has promised His judgment would come for many years. I doubt it will be tonight."

"And if it is?"

"Then it is a risk I am willing to take."

Noah started to answer, then stopped. You could tell he wanted to say more, but you could also tell it would do no good.

Ham waited another moment before turning and walking away. "Good evening, Father." As he left he brushed past me. "I shall see you in the morning."

I watched as Noah wilted like someone had let all the air out of his tires. Then, ever so softly, he said, "God have mercy upon you, my son . . . upon all of us."

I stood there, trying to make up my mind. Should I stay with Noah? Or should I follow his son? Then there was Gita and all the people back at the control panel. They were probably worried. Another wave of laughter and music floated from the hilltop. Well, one thing was clear—there would never be another chance like this. And since I was here and there wasn't much happening on the boat—and since all the action seemed to be over at the party—I turned and ran to catch up with Ham.

Chapter Seven

FOLDING DIMENSIONS

J
E
N
N
I
F
E
R

"Uh . . . Jen?"

"Yeah, Jesse?"

"WHAT'S HAPPENING?"

I couldn't help smiling. I knew Jesse wanted to be all cool and manly. But I also knew he was terrified. Who wouldn't be? I certainly was, at least the first time I did this. Come to think of it, every time. Let's face it, traveling through space so fast that all the stars are blurring past you like some old *Star Wars* movie will do that to a person.

"JENNY!"

I turned to see him floating beside me. Except for the yelling, he almost pulled off the calm and cool thing, though there was the fact that those beautiful blue eyes were as wide as dinner plates.

"Relax," I said, "we're just folding dimensions."

"FOLDING DIMENSIONS! ARE YOU—" He caught himself, cleared his throat, and tried again—cooler, calmer. "Sorry, this is all just a little—FOLDING DIMENSIONS! ARE YOU CRAZY?" Again he shrugged. "Sorry."

I chuckled. No one had really told him what to suspect. And I suppose it served him right for jumping in without being asked. Then again it was sweet the way he tried to save me. Either way I figured it was time to explain what was happening to us. How the universe was like a piece of paper. And instead of traveling across it from one point to another, the dimensional folder simply folded the universe so the two points were next to each other. Of course we still had to cross through a few extra dimensions to get there. "But other than that," I said, "it's perfectly normal."

"PERFEC—perfectly normal?" (He was getting better.)

"That's right and we're just about through the first part."

"*First* part?" He swallowed, this time sounding calm, though he might have been more convincing if his voice hadn't cracked. Poor guy.

I explained. "The first part is pretty normal. Well, normal in that we can at least understand it."

"These are shooting stars," he said.

I nodded. "But the next couple parts will get so weird and confusing that, well, Gita says it's best just to close our eyes—you know, so we don't freak."

"It gets worse?"

I shook my head. "Just weird."

I don't think that helped him relax. After a moment of looking around, he asked, "What's that sound?"

I strained to listen. "I don't hear—"

"Are those voices? Is that . . . singing?"

I nodded. "Oh, yeah."

We both paused to listen. Finally he spoke. "I don't understand the words, they're not in English, but it's, it's . . ."

"Beautiful?" I said.

"Yeah." He started to smile. The music was so gorgeous he didn't have a choice. Come to think of it, neither did I. It's hard to explain, but imagine the purest voices ever. Now, imagine them swirling and overlapping each other but without ever losing their intensity. Instead, each voice becomes more vivid. Somehow by combining with the others, they grow and blossom, each working with the others to become more beautiful on their own and more beautiful together.

I looked over to Jesse and saw moisture filling his eyes. Who could blame him? It was *that* beautiful. He spotted me and gave them a quick, embarrassed swipe. But the tears just kept coming, for both of us. Not because we were sad, but because the music was so full of love. And it wasn't just in our ears. Somehow it was also soaking into our bodies, our minds . . . and our hearts.

"This is stupid," he said, glancing away and giving his eyes another swipe.

I nodded and grinned, wiping my own. He saw me and grinned back, which made my heart swell toward him all the more. I don't know if it was the music, or him, or both. But I really did appreciate him.

The voices grew bigger. Not louder like in volume, but bigger as in fuller. There weren't more voices, they just filled up more of the space around us . . . and inside us.

Then came the first flash of light—as bright as the sun but not blinding. And more white than light. It was all around us, like the music. And, like the music, you could actually feel its brightness, its whiteness growing inside.

"Wow," Jesse whispered.

I nodded because that was really all you could say.

There was another flash, and then another, faster and closer. No, not closer . . . deeper.

"This is the part where we're supposed to close our eyes," I said.

The flashes came faster until they were one, continuous light.

"This is incredible," Jesse said. "I mean, it's so bright, but it doesn't hurt your eyes. And it's inside. Jen, look! It's inside you!"

I glanced down and, sure enough, it was like I was glowing inside. And when I looked back up to Jesse, I broke out laughing. "You too! *You're* glowing!"

He looked down and was as surprised as me.

"Okay," I said, "but we really have to close our eyes now."

"Why?" Jesse asked, raising his hand and examining the glow in his fingers.

"Because it gets weird."

It was pretty obvious he wasn't going to listen, so acting as an example, I titled back my head and closed my own eyes. That's when I felt the softness.

It brushed against my face, as soft as feathers. Like the music and light, it completely surrounded me. As it did, everything grew even brighter and whiter. And somehow, this was hardest to explain, but the music became the light. Or the light became the music. And they both became the softness. Everything was the same and everything was everywhere . . . outside, inside, in my thoughts, in my emotions, until, suddenly—

"Ahhh!" Jesse shouted.

My eyes popped open to see what was wrong. But he wasn't beside me. Instead, he floated eight or ten feet below me and seemed to be falling further away every second. No. He wasn't falling. I was rising . . . into light above me. Light that kept getting whiter and whiter, brighter and brighter, along with the light inside me. I was glowing in the exact same brightness as the light around me.

"Jesse?" I shouted. "What are you doing? Come up here."

"It's hot!" he yelled. Like me, he was still glowing, but not as bright, just like the light around him wasn't as bright. He raised his arm into the brighter light above him and the inside of his fingers suddenly flickered with red fire. He yanked it back and shouted, "It's burning! What's going on?"

"I don't know," I called back. "I'm okay. Try it again."

He tried again and again the fingers and the upper part of his hand seemed to catch fire. "It burns!" he shouted.

I shook my head, not understanding, as I continued to rise.

"Jen! Wait up. Hang on a sec."

By now I was even farther above him in much brighter light. I tried stopping. I tried turning and dropping back down to him, but I didn't know how. It wasn't like swimming where I had water or something I could paddle against. It was just music and light that kept getting brighter and brighter outside of me and inside.

Jesse tried again, raising both arms. And they both caught fire. It was like the light inside him couldn't stand the brighter light above him. Like he had to stay in the same brightness that was around him because if he tried to go higher, the brighter light would set him on fire.

I started to panic. What were we supposed to do? How could I help Jesse? What would happen if—

Suddenly, the voices in and around me sang in English. Or at least in a language my mind understood: "Daughter, you are safe."

Safe? I thought. *How can I be safe when my friend is—*

"The King's daughter is always safe."

It was like they read my mind. And their words were even more confusing. Dad was an archeologist, not a king. *Who*—I tried thinking out my thoughts, but they beat me to it.

"We are the servants."

Servants? I thought.

"Of the King, your Father."

My father?

"JEN!" Jesse shouted. I looked back down. He was way below now—still trying to rise, still catching fire and pulling back.

My friend, I thought.

"—may come no farther. The purity will destroy him."

You mean the light?

"The purity."

I tilted my head and looked up. The light just kept getting whiter and whiter. *What about me?* I thought.

"You are perfection. Perfection may enter all purity."

Perfection? I'm not perfect.

"There is no imperfection in you."

There's plenty wrong, trust me.

"No. The Pure has made you pure. He sees nothing wrong with you."

That's crazy. I'm not pure.

"He sees nothing wrong with you, only what is missing."

But—

"The Pure has made you pure, so you are pure. In time He will heal the missing."

"Jen!"

I looked back down to Jesse. He was almost out of sight.

What about my friend?

"He must close his eyes to what he would see."

But—

"By closing his eyes, he will pass through."

You just said the purity will destroy him.

"He may pass through, not up. There is a difference. He must close his eyes. He must focus on our song."

Not being in a position to argue, I yelled down to him, "Jesse, close your eyes!"

He shouted, "Are you nuts! How's that going to—"

"Just do it! Close your eyes and listen to the music."

He didn't answer.

"Jesse!"

"All right, all right." He wasn't happy, but it sounded like he was going to give it a try. Not that he had much choice.

"And you, daughter," the voices sang. "To join him and pass through, close your eyes as well."

Before I could answer, I felt a gentle pressure on my eyelids, like the feathers were brushing against them. I could have fought back and resisted, but I let them close.

Immediately, I heard Jesse's voice. This time beside me. "Jen?"

"Right here," I said.

"What was—"

"I'll explain later. Keep your eyes shut."

"They are."

"Good, because we're not through this yet."

"What do you mean?"

I could already feel the heat against my face and saw the red flickering against my eyelids. "Just keep them closed," I repeated. "This is where it gets freaky."

Chapter Eight

INTO THE NIGHT

J
A
K
E

Following Ham and his wife, whose name was Phelmona, wasn't as hard as you'd think. Actually, it was pretty easy, since they couldn't see or hear me. It was like I was an invisible ghost beside them—but without all the BooOOOOooo-ing, haunting, and chain rattling. Still, even though I wasn't real to them, they sure seemed real to me, which explains all my staggering through brush, stumbling over fallen logs, and

ROLL,

       ROLL,

              ROLLING . . .

down ravines—while enjoying the minimum daily require-
ments of twisted ankles and bruised body parts. Okay, so
I'm not the world's greatest outdoorsman. But put me on
a sidewalk with a skateboard and I'd shut down these Paul
Bunyan types any day of the week. Unfortunately, I'd left
my skateboard at home and didn't see many sidewalks in
this part of the woods. But being the tough guy I am, I was
able to pick myself up and keep on going.

"Shh," Ham held up his hand and we came to a stop.
"Did you hear something?"

I caught my breath, thinking I'd blown my cover,
until Phelmona pointed into the growing darkness. "Over
there."

We turned to see a couple deer coming down a path;
a doe and a buck with huge antlers. (*Note to self: Avoid
deer antlers, they're a lot like the bull horns.*) Not far behind
them, on the same path, were two big wolves, and behind
them a pair of goats, and behind them some black growling
somethings that blended into the darkness. (*Note to self:
Avoid black, growling somethings too.*)

"It's the animals," Ham whispered. "They're coming."

"Without anyone going to get them?" Phelmona said.

Ham nodded. "Without any *human* getting them."

We watched in silent awe. To think I was the only
twenty-first century person to see this. Imagine the excitement when I get back home. Imagine the fame, the glory.
Imagine the magazine covers. This, of course, led to even
deeper thoughts and concerns:

For autographs did I want to use my whole name,
Jake Mackenzie, or just my initials **JM**? (Probably initials, 'cause with so many fans I don't want to get writer's

cramp.) And what about a greeting? *Best Wishes?* Naw, too formal. *Forever yours?* No way—well, unless she's cute. Decisions, decisions.

"We must forget the party." Phelmona's voice drew my thoughts off me (which was no problem 'cause I'm sure they'd return). "We must warn my brother and cousins."

Ham nodded. "Hopefully they will listen."

"Why would they not?"

"The Lord said only our family will be saved."

She looked at him a moment then turned away. You could tell she wasn't happy in a big way.

"But we shall try." Ham grabbed her hand and they started forward. "We shall try."

The good news was my twisted ankles and bruised body parts weren't a major problem. The better news was that after only a few more minutes of staggering and falling (but no **ROLL, ROLL, ROLLING**), we finally made it to the top of the hill.

The place had gone crazy . . . literally. It was like some ultracool carnival, at least at first glance. But as we joined the crowd, things got to looking (and smelling) a lot more uncool.

Let's start with the smell. I'm not an expert at booze or anything like that (why people want to drink stuff that tastes like gasoline is beyond me), but the whole place reeked with it. Not that everyone was drunk—I'm sure there was a sober baby or two—but people were stumbling around, cussing, fighting, and making out right there in public. I don't want to be a prude or anything, but even before some guy staggered over and

HURL-ed

all over my shoes, I was thinking things were pretty disgusting . . . almost as bad as the stuff you see on TV.

Almost.

In some ways it reminded me of those college parties you see in the movies. Actually, in a lot of ways. How weird—it always looked so fun in the movies. But in real life, forget it. The place was gross and creepy—a definite "No Sale" in the fun department.

With all the bumping, jostling, (and **HURL**-ing), it was hard to keep up with Ham and Phelmona. Pretty soon we got separated, but that was okay. There was plenty to see. Off to my right there was a bunch of cheering and shouting. It couldn't be any worse than where I was, so I checked it out.

I was wrong. It was worse.

At first I thought it was a wrestling or boxing match. And it was, kind of. But when I got closer I saw the fighters weren't using gloves. Who needs gloves when you've got knives and swords? It was like some video game—complete with blood, cut off limbs, and gory sound effects. Only this was real.

I felt my stomach getting queasy. So this is what they did for entertainment. Talk about gross. But as I looked around, it dawned on me that in some way, things really weren't that different from back home—at least the stuff you see in the movies—the cussing, the drinking, the sex, the violence. Yeah, I get it's not the same as real life, but I also get that it's as close as you can come. And if folks can't "enjoy" watching it in the movies, they can always bring it into their living rooms and watch it on DVD. I could get all judgmental about the people, here. But, really, was there that much difference between them and us?

And just when I thought I'd seen it all, I began seeing a lot more . . .

Chapter Nine

HELLO, 1961

**J
E
N
N
I
F
E
R**

"What's happening now?" Jesse asked.

"Are your eyes shut?"

"Yeah," he sighed, "but not liking it."

By now all the light had faded, along with the music and feathers. Now there was only blackness and that red flickering against our closed eyes.

"Where are we now?" he asked.

"Gita said it's like a lower dimension."

"Lower dimension?"

"Well, not lower than back home. Back home we live in three dimensions. But we're lower here than we were with all that light and music." I'd barely finished the sentence before I heard faint growling off in the distance.

"Jen?"

"Yeah, I hear it too," I said.

"Are those . . . animals?"

"Not exactly." The growling grew louder. Along with it came that awful clicking and clacking noise, like the chortling sound crows make. I felt myself growing cold and took a deep breath. I was in no mood for another battle with that winged shadow thing that I kept running into.

"I'm opening my eyes," Jesse said.

"No, don't!"

The noise grew louder, closer.

"I'm not hanging around getting attacked by something I don't even know what it is."

"Jess, no!"

Before he could answer, we heard another sound—a woman's voice calling a name:

"Billy!"

The growling faded. So did the red flickering. It dissolved into what felt like normal daylight.

"Billy, lunch!"

"That's it," Jesse said. "I'm going to look."

"Yeah, okay," I said. "I think it's safe."

I opened my eyes and stepped off the dimensional folder. We were standing on a sidewalk in the middle of an old-fashioned neighborhood. On the porch of the white, two-story house stood a young woman calling, "William Mackenzie! You get home this very minute! Do you hear me?"

Jesse and I traded looks. "'William Mackenzie,'" he said. "That's your dad's name."

I nodded and looked back to the woman.

He continued. "If she's calling to your dad, and he's her son . . ."

I finished his thought. "That would make her my Grandma?" I whispered, "That's Grandma Mackenzie."

"Billy!"

I felt a lump growing in my throat. "She's so young," I said. "So beautiful."

"We really are back in 1961, aren't we," Jesse said.

I nodded and swallowed at the lump that kept getting bigger. I bent over and scooped up the dimensional folder, which had stopped flashing. I handed it to Jesse who folded it up and slipped it into his coat. I looked back over to the lady, cleared my voice and finally called out, "Grandma?"

The woman turned to us with a startled look. "Land's sakes, where did you two come from?"

"Are you my—"

Jesse coughed loudly to catch my attention.

I got the message and changed questions. "Are you Mrs. Mackenzie? Mrs. . . . Doris Mackenzie?"

She shaded her eyes against the sun. "Why, yes. Do I know you?"

"We're, uh, um . . ."

Jesse came to my rescue. "We're brand new to the neighborhood."

I nodded. He definitely had a point.

"Oh," the woman smiled warmly. "You must be the family that moved into the Peterson place."

"Uh, right," Jesse said. It was a lie and before I could stop him, he added, "I'm Jesse and this here is Jennifer."

She stepped further out onto the porch. She closed the screen door behind her and pushed aside her bangs like she always did when she was alive. Of course they were a beautiful, chestnut brown, not the gray I remembered. Then there was her smile. I loved that smile. She'd been gone over half my life but I never forgot it. I felt my heart leap and break all at the same time.

"Well, it's a pleasure to meet you Jesse and Jennifer . . . ?" She let the question hang in the air, waiting for an answer.

"Johnson," Jesse said at the same time I said, "Smith."

She smiled, "I'm sorry?"

"Smith," Jesse said at the same time I said, "Johnson."

Her smile wilted slightly.

"Mixed family," I said.

"Divorced," Jesse added.

Grandma's fading smile turned to a deep frown of sympathy. "Oh my poor dears." She stepped off the porch to give us a little hug. "I'm so sorry—so very, very sorry. It must be a terrible ordeal for you."

I appreciated the hug, but making such a big deal out of divorce surprised me. Half the kids in my class come from divorced families. Then again, as Jesse said, we were back in 1961. I guess times really had changed.

After the hug she continued. "You tell your mother, if there's anything I can do to help, please let me know."

"We will," I said.

"Thanks," Jesse added.

"You are most certainly welcome." Then, looking up the street, the slightest trace of worry crossed her face. "I'm wondering if you two darlings would do me a favor?"

"What's that?" I asked.

"My little boy, Billy? Sometimes he gets to playing so hard he loses all track of time."

I couldn't help smiling at how she had just described my dad. Some things never change.

"Would you be dears and go next door to the Simons' there and tell him to come home? It's getting close to supper time and he needs to get washed up."

I caught my breath and thought, *Simons, wasn't that mom's maiden name? Of course, she and Dad had grown up together.*

"Sure," I heard Jesse answer. "No problem."

"Thank you," Grandma said. "He's in the backyard. Can't miss him. He'll be the one covered head to toe with dirt." Shaking her head, she chuckled. "That boy just loves to dig."

Jesse and I traded looks. It's true, some things *never* change.

"Well," she said, starting back to the house, "you be sure to greet your parents for me. And tell your mama"— she arrived at the porch and turned to us—"tell her I'm going to bake you up a nice apple pie."

"Oh, there's no need," Jesse said.

"Nonsense, it's only good manners." She opened the screen door. "Now be sure to send Billy home, you hear?"

"Yes, ma'am."

She nodded, gave that little smile of hers, then disappeared into the house, closing the door behind her.

For a moment I just stood there, unable to breathe.
Finally, Jesse spoke. "Wow."

I took a deep breath. That said it all. We started down
the sidewalk.

"It's like watching one of those old black-and-white TV
shows," Jesse said. "Everybody so homey and friendly."

I nodded.

"Did you notice something else?"

"What's that?"

"What parent would trust two complete strangers to
send her kid home?"

"It's true," I said. "Things really were different."

We arrived in front of the house next door and came
to a stop.

"So what do we do?" I said. "Just walk into their backyard, without asking?"

Jesse shrugged, "I suppose." He started forward. "And
hope we don't get shot."

"No worries there," I said. "It is 1961. Besides I know
these people."

"The Simons?" he asked.

"Yeah, that was my mom's maiden name. And I know
she and Dad grew up together."

"Cool," Jesse said.

We crossed through the front yard and came to a
white picket gate at the side of the house. We opened it
and walked to the back. It looked like any other backyard,
except it was almost twice as big as mine in California.
Near the back fence, under a maple tree, was a big pile of
sand. A cute, little boy in glasses and about seven years old
was furiously digging into it. I felt my legs get just a little

rubbery. Was it possible? Was this really my dad? Sensing my unsteadiness, Jesse reached out and took my arm.

"Be careful," the boy called to someone on the other side of the sand pile. He tried to sound strong and commanding, though his squeaky voice and slight lisp made him all the cuter. "We don't want to hurt the dinosaur bones."

"Okay, Billy," a tiny girl's voice replied.

"Museums don't like hurt dinosaur bones, you know."

"Okay."

He continued digging. The two of us just stood there watching. He had a small kid's shovel and wasn't making much progress, but that didn't stop him from attacking the hill with everything he had.

Jesse was the first to speak; a good thing, because I could barely breathe, let alone talk. "Hey there," he said.

The little boy glanced up. "Hello." He kept digging.

"Are you Billy?"

"Uh-huh."

We traded looks. My knees grew weaker.

Jesse continued. "There's, uh, somebody here who would like to meet you."

He kept digging.

Jesse gave me a look, then a little nudge before I finally cleared my throat. "Hi," I croaked. "My name is," I swallowed. "My name is Jennifer.

He stopped digging a moment and looked at me.

"Hi," I repeated.

"Hello."

We stared at each other in the world's second most awkward pause. (I'll get to the first in just a moment.)

I knew I should say something, but for the life of me, I couldn't think what. He saved me the trouble.

"You're pretty," he said, then returned to his digging.

I almost broke down right then and there. In all his life, Daddy had never complimented me; not like that. Oh, sure, for good grades and stuff, but never on my looks.

"Billy?"

I looked up and saw a five-year-old girl appear over the top of the sand pile. She was wearing overalls, had short blonde hair, and a face smudged with dirt. When she saw us, she slowed to a stop.

Dad paused and in his most exasperated, grown-up voice said, "What is it now, Debbie?"

I gasped.

"You okay?" Jesse asked.

I tried to talk, but no words came.

He quickly put the pieces together. "Debbie . . . was that your mother's name?"

I could only nod, my eyes welling with tears.

"Are you all right?" the little boy asked me.

Jesse answered. "She's just a little tired—we've been on a long trip." Turning to the girl, he asked, "Is your name, are you Debbie Simons?"

She took a step backward and Billy immediately came to her defense. "Is she in trouble? She hasn't done anything, she's been with me all morning."

"No, no, she isn't in trouble," Jesse said.

I wiped my eyes, trying to get a better view. They were so cute together, my seven-year-old father, protecting my little five-year-old mother.

"Well, Debbie," he finally said. "We better get back to work. Not much light before nightfall."

"Okay, boss." Mom turned and started back over the hill.

"No wait!" I said. "Don't go!"

She turned and they both stared at me. And I just stared at them. Remember that second most awkward pause in human history? Well, this was the first.

But it didn't last long.

At first I thought the shadows moving on the ground came from the wind blowing the tree branches over our heads. It made perfect sense, except there was no wind. And the tree branches were not blowing. But the shadows were definitely moving. It was like they had minds of their own as they swarmed across the ground toward one another, almost like they were alive. And for good reason. They were alive! I'd seen them before, back at camp—this is how the creepy winged creature formed.

Jesse heard me gasp. "What's wrong?" he asked.

"Don't you see it?"

"See what?"

There was no time to explain. The shadows had nearly connected. "Dad!" I shouted. "Run!"

The little fellow looked at me blankly. So did the girl.

"Run!" I broke from Jesse's side and raced toward them. "Get out of here! Go!" Jesse shouted something after me but I didn't hear. I waved my arms running at them like a crazy person. "Run! Run!"

Mom screamed and started off, which is exactly what I wanted. But not Dad. He had to be a hero. He tried protecting her by swinging his little shovel at me. I dodged it once, then twice. I heard the awful clicking and clacking sound and looked back to the shadow. It had completely formed into the winged creature and was rising off the ground.

"Back!" Dad swung at me again. "Back!

I managed to grab his shovel. He hung on as I pulled him into my face and roared, "RUN!"

That did the trick. Hero or no hero, Dad took off.

Mom was in the lead, Dad not far behind as I followed behind them, still waving my arms and yelling. When we reached the side gate I heard what sounded like a bed sheet or a sail snapping in the wind. I heard it again and knew the shadow thing was airborne. It was flapping its wings and heading straight toward us.

"Jen! What are you doing?" Jesse was somewhere behind, shouting at me to stop, but it didn't matter. I had to save my parents. We entered the front yard, Mom and Dad just a couple steps ahead of me. There was another flap of wings, closer. And then another. It was almost on top of us.

Memories of Gita's voice surfaced. *You have the authority. With Jesus Christ, you have the authority.*

It's true. I'd used that authority at the airport just a few days ago and it worked. It was scary, but it had worked. I'd gone toe-to-toe with the thing and won. So, with her words fresh in my memory, I whirled around to face it—its grotesque beak and eyes, those giant wings—just a few feet behind me.

"Stop!" I shouted. "In the name of Jesus Christ, I order you to stop!"

The thing froze. It reared back its leathery head and hissed trying to scare me. But I had the authority and I was going to use it. "I command you, in the name of—"

"Debbie, look out!"

I heard the screech of brakes and spun around to see Mom and Dad in the middle of the street, a beat up station wagon coming straight at them. *Coming straight at Mom!* Before I could move, Dad leaped between the car and Mom, shoving her out of the way. It missed her but hit him, head on. I could hear the sound of steel as it slammed into his little body, the thump of his little head hit the pavement . . . and Mom's screams as the front wheel of the car ran over him.

Chapter Ten

A REAL KNOCKOUT

J
A
K
E

So there I was, stuck in a holograph of Noah's times (which in some ways was no different from our times) when I spotted that wide-eyed, innocent blonde girl I'd seen earlier. She was looking all over and calling out names that sounded like, "Bennak? Rennai?" By the way she clapped and whistled it was like she was looking for dogs or pets or something. "Bennak, Rennai, where are you, boys?" She seemed pretty worried and by the way she staggered back and forth she also looked pretty drunk. And if you couldn't tell by the way she staggered, you could tell by the way her breath smelled as she wobbled past.

(So much for innocent.)

Unfortunately all the jerks around her, who were equally unsober, were busy being . . . well, jerks. They kept reaching and grabbing for her, and every time she pushed them away, they just laughed and grabbed at her all the more. I'm guessing trying to help her find whatever she'd lost was not their top priority.

I don't want to get all sentimental or anything, but it really bugged me to see how they treated her. It's true, she wasn't exactly Miss Morality, but one look into her eyes and you could also see she was this scared, lost, little girl. She got even more scared when a big bruiser of a guy, the size of a Ford pickup, pushed his way through the crowd, yelling what must have been her name:

"Enthal!"

Everybody parted like the Red Sea as the big boy approached.

"What are you doing, spending time with these cockroaches?" he shouted.

"I wasn't," she cried. "I was looking for the puppies."

He glared at her and her eyes widened in fear.

He glared at her some more and she started shaking.

One of the cockroaches stepped up to him and said, "We was just helpin' her, Naalamachelruha." (Hey, don't blame me, I didn't name him.) "We was tryin' to find her little mutts and makin' sure she don't get hurt by all these other despicable types." He motioned to the crowd, which showed their appreciation by booing and yelling at the cockroach.

"Silence!" Big Bruiser shouted.

Everyone stopped like he'd just clicked their pause buttons. Then he raised his giant arm, the type you find on the cover of any muscle magazine. And, just like that, all the cockroaches scampered off. All but one.

"You don't own her," the one said.

"That's right." (Okay, all but two.)

"You tell him." (Make that three.)

"AARGH!" Bruiser aargh-ed.

"See, ya!" Number Three cried.

"I'm out of here!" Number Two agreed.

Like I said, all but one scampered off. And he was either very stupid or very drunk or very both. Because when Bruiser Boy grabbed Enthal and carried her off, the little guy grabbed a rock and attacked, which was a bit like a mosquito attacking an elephant—until the little guy scampered up Naalamachelruha's leg and waist and finally onto his shoulders where he sat and began

thud, thud, thudd-ing

the man's head.

The big boy got the message and began spinning and slamming into various walls trying to throw him off. But the little dude hung on and kept pounding. By now everyone was laughing and it might have been funny except for Enthal. Since Naalamachelruha had never dropped her, she was spinning and slamming into the very same walls he was. Of course she screamed in pain and terror but that only made the crowd laugh harder.

Not me. Look, I'm no hero or anything, but the poor girl was getting it pretty bad. So, before I could stop myself, I ran into the fight. (I know, I know, on the intelligence scale of 1 to 10, it was about a minus 3.) Anyway,

I threw my self at brusier boy, but because he was just a holographic image of a historical event, he felt nothing.

Unfortunately, because those images were so realistic to my brain, I felt plenty! I don't want to be a crybaby, but if you've ever wondered what a fly felt like hitting the windshield of a semitruck, drop me an e-mail and I'll explain—though I'm not sure which hospital you should send it to. After hitting him, I kinda slid to the ground in a daze and watched as bruiser boy finally threw off his unwanted hitchhiker.

That was great for him . . . not so great for me. Why? Let me count the ways:

1. The little hitchhiker flew straight toward me.
2. The little hitchhiker refused to let go of the rock.
3. Instead of a nonstop flight to the ground, the little hitchhiker and his not-so-little rock had a slight layover . . . against the side of my

THUD

head.

About that e-mail? Forget the hospital's address, just look up heaven's.

Chapter Eleven

HALF-TRUTHS

J
E
N
N
I
F
E
R

"DAD!"

I'd barely knelt down to his little body before some-one grabbed me and was trying to pull me away. "Get back. I'm a doctor, let me in." It was the driver of the car, an older man. And he was really shaken. "Please, let me in."

Jesse was also beside me pulling. "Jen."

I let the doctor in but kept staring at Dad's unmoving body. I couldn't believe what was happening. It was a nightmare.

"Son?" the doctor kept saying. "Son, can you hear me?"

But Dad just laid there, his eyes closed. I wasn't even sure he was breathing. I heard another sound. Crying. I looked up and saw little Debbie. She stood to the side, hand to her mouth, tears streaming down her face.

"Mom . . ." my voice cracked. I struggled to my feet. "It's okay." I held out my arms to her. "He'll be okay, sweetheart." She took a step backward. "It's okay."

"What happened?" I turned to see Grandma Mackenzie racing toward us. "Billy?" You could see the fear in her face. "Billy?" She arrived, pushing past me and joining the doctor.

"He came out of nowhere," the doctor said. "I was driving and he just—"

"I saw it all!"

We turned to see an older woman approach—skinny, pinch-faced, wisps of gray hair hanging in her face. She pointed directly at me. "This girl, she was chasing them. Running him right out into the street."

Other neighbors arrived, crowding in to see what happened.

"Billy . . ." Grandma was on her knees, starting to weep. "Billy . . ."

"Someone call an ambulance," the doctor shouted to the neighbors. "Call an ambulance."

"Billy . . . Billy . . ."

The pinch-faced woman glared at me. "She was

shouting at him. Chasing him right into the street like she wanted this to happen!"

"Will someone call an ambulance!"

By now everyone had turned to me. I threw a look to Jesse who was as confused as I was. That's when I noticed the shadow. It had been a perfectly clear day just a minute ago, but now a cloud hovered in the sky. I tilted back my head and looked up. It wasn't a cloud. It was the winged creature. It circled high above us, blocking the sun. It didn't come any closer. It didn't have to. The damage was already done.

"Where are you two from?" someone was asking Jesse.

"We, uh . . ."

"They're not from around here," another said.

"Out into the street like she wanted it to happen," the old lady repeated.

Above us I heard the creature's clicking and chortling. Maybe it was my imagination, but it almost sounded like laughter.

· · · · · · · ·

Twenty minutes later we were sitting in the back of a police car. No matter what we did I couldn't seem to get warm. The officer, a skinny, bald guy, had found a blanket and put it around me.

"Is she, like, under arrest?" Jesse asked.

"No, son."

"Then you really can't hold her, can you? I mean without a search warrant or something."

The officer looked away so Jesse couldn't see his smile.

I whispered, "You learn that on TV?"

"Hey," he whispered back, "you can learn lots on TV."

Finally the officer answered. "I suppose I could let her join *them*." He motioned to all the neighbors still gathered outside—with more than a few throwing death glares in my direction.

Jesse got the message. "No, I think we'll stay in here and help as long as we can."

"I thought so."

"Any word on my da—uh, the little boy?" I asked. The ambulance had left a few minutes earlier and Dad was still unconscious.

The officer sighed. "Pretty severe head injury. Doesn't look good."

I threw a nervous glance to Jesse.

The officer nodded up the street. "So you recently moved into the Peterson house."

"Right," Jesse said. "That's right."

"Hmm," the officer said. "I wonder why there isn't any furniture inside?"

"Oh, that," Jesse cleared his throat. "Mom, she's not that much into furniture."

"Hmm," he repeated. "Just one more question, at least for now."

"What's that?" we asked in unison.

He motioned up the street. "You know the Peterson house up there?"

"Uh-huh," we said in perfect unison.

He nodded down the street. "It's actually down there."

We swallowed in perfect unison.

Before we could get into any more trouble another officer called. "Anderson, come over here."

He pulled his head out of the car and turned to join his partner, but not before leaving behind a friendly suggestion. "Don't go anywhere and don't do anything. We've got some talking to do."

I leaned back in the seat and blew out a breath.

"You okay?" Jesse asked.

"Other than getting thrown into jail for killing my dad, yeah, I guess I'm all right. What about you?"

He didn't answer. When I looked at him I could see something was up. "What's wrong?

He shook his head.

"No, tell me, what else is wrong?"

"It's just . . . if your dad dies while he's still a kid before you're born . . ."

It slowly dawned on me. "Then I wouldn't be born."

He nodded.

"I would never have existed."

More in the nodding department.

"Well, then, we're okay."

"Why do you say that?"

I scoffed. "Because I'm here." I pulled my arm out from under the blanket. "See, I'm—" That's when I stopped and stared.

"Oh, no," Jesse said.

"Oh, brother," I groaned.

I raised my arm for a better look. I brought my hand to my face. Well, what was left of my hand. It was still there and everything. Four fingers, a thumb, a palm, all accounted for. Except.

"It's all misty," Jesse said and reached out to take my hand. But instead of touching it, his own hand passed through it like it was fog.

Chapter Twelve

DISAPPEARING ACT

**J
E
N
N
I
F
E
R**

"What do we do?" I cried.

"All right, okay," Jesse said, doing his best not to hyper-ventilate. "First of all we don't panic. Whatever we do, don't panic, all right? Just relax and whatever you do, let me repeat: **do . . . not . . . panic.**"

"I'm not panicking."

"Not you," he said. "Me."

I nodded as he took a deep breath to calm himself. And then another. I appreciated his concern. I would have appreciated it more if he had a plan . . . because when I pulled off the rest of the blanket we saw it wasn't just my hand that was disappearing, it was my arm, my body, even my clothes—*everything* was turning to mist!

Jesse snapped his fingers. "I've got it! This is all about your father, right?"

"Right."

"I mean if he dies it's like you never existed, right?"

"Right."

"So all we have to do is go to the hospital and save his life!"

"Righ—Wait a minute, how do we do that?"

"Didn't I tell you, I want to be a doctor?"

"You're fourteen."

"I watch all the medical shows.

I gave him a look.

"I'm open for a better idea."

I had none.

"Okay, first, we have to get out of here." He turned and crawled from the car. "We'll make up the rest as we go along."

"Make it up?"

He nodded. "Improvise."

I wasn't crazy about the idea, but when he reached down to tenderly take my hand and gently help me out, who could resist? Of course it would have been more romantic if his hand didn't pass straight through mine.

I'd barely stepped outside when the pinch-faced woman shouted from across the street, "What are you doing?"

Jesse and I looked at each other nervously.

"They're trying to escape!" someone cried.

Escape sounded like a pretty good idea (particularly when they started toward us) so we took off running. It didn't matter where, just as long as it was in the opposite direction.

"You there!" One of the policemen shouted. He was about a hundred pounds overweight and looked more like a giant marshmallow in uniform than an actual cop. Though he did have one thing in his favor—a gun.

"Stop right there!" he shouted.

Normally, as a law-abiding citizen, I would have obeyed. But another person also weighed in. Well, not really a person. More like a shadow. I heard it cackle and chortle. When I looked up, I saw the winged creature begin diving toward us. We had to get out of the open and take cover.

"That way!" I shouted. We turned and cut through somebody's front yard.

"Stop!" The policeman started after us.

I heard the shadow thing flap its wings.

We threw open a side gate and ran into the backyard. We followed a broken down fence all the way to the alley. The yard across the alley was fenced in, but the next one was open. We raced to it and cut through that yard to the next street.

The policeman was still behind us, though running out of air. "Stop! (*Pant-pant.*) I order you to (*gasp-gasp*) stop!" The winged creature had risen back into the air, obviously trying to cut us off.

We reached the street and spotted a boxy-looking, panel truck with an old-fashioned milk bottle painted on its side. Some guy dressed in white had just stepped from it. He carried a wire basket filled with the same old-fashioned bottles.

"There!" Jesse pointed at the truck and we ran toward it. The sunlight around us shimmered then turned to shadow. The creature was directly overhead. It would not give up.

Neither would the policeman. "Stop (*wheeze*) right (*pant*) there (*gasp*)!"

We arrived at the truck and I scrambled inside. Jesse followed, scooting behind the wheel. He grabbed the gear shift and began grinding away.

"What are you doing?" I shouted.

"Looking for first! It's here somewhere!"

He found it. The truck lurched forward and we were off, not without one or two well-wishers bidding us a fond farewell:

"Hey, that's my truck!"

"St—(*wheeze-wheeze, pant-pant, gasp-gasp*)—op!"

I turned to Jesse. "This is totally illegal! Stealing a truck is bad, really bad!"

"So is killing your dad, running from the police, and"—he nodded at me—"disappearing!"

I glanced down. By now I was more invisible than visible . . . and getting worse by the second!

I heard a squeal of brakes and looked up as Jesse swerved hard to the left, then the right. We'd just shot through a red light as more cars skidded and horns honked.

"Where'd you learn to drive?" I shouted.

"The desert!"

I heard the crash of glass and metal behind us. "Not many stop lights in the desert?"

A stuck horn blared.

"Not many."

"Thought so." I reached into my pocket and pulled out my cell phone.

"What are you doing?"

"Finding the nearest hospital. Where they took Dad."

"I don't think that's going to work."

I looked at him.

"It's 1961. No such thing as Google."

I glanced at the blank screen. "Or cell phones," I sighed.

Jesse leaned toward me. "What?"

"They don't have cell phones either."

"What?" he said. "You're going to have to speak up."

It was only then I realized that not only was my body fading . . . so was my voice.

Jesse cranked the wheel hard to the left and we shot across traffic toward a gas station. We bounced up over the curb and raced toward a head-on with the gas pumps. I screamed as he hit the brakes and we screeched to a stop, missing them by just inches.

Jesse threw open the door. "Stay here," he shouted, "I'm going inside to get directions."

"Not on your life," I said. "I'm coming with." Before he could protest, I slid across the seat and joined him. The moment I stepped outside I was hit with what felt like an Arctic blast. It blew right through me.

Jesse must have heard me gasp, because he turned and squinted against the sunlight, trying to see me. "You okay?"

"The wind," I shivered. "it's s-s-so cold."

"What wind?" He looked around. "There's no wind. There's barely a breeze."

"Then w-w-why—" I was too cold to finish.

"It's blowing through you!" he said. "It's blowing straight through you!"

By now I was shaking so hard I could only nod. It made sense. If I was barely there, anything could pass through me, even the wind. Trying to protect me, Jesse took off his jacket and wrapped it around my shoulders. But it fell right through me to the ground.

I kept shaking, but now as much from the cold as from fear.

He picked up the coat and tried again. This time he held it in place. I'm sure he looked stupid, holding a jacket out in mid air, but it was the only way he could protect me. Even though I was terrified, my heart swelled with gratitude.

Another shadow passed over the sun. I looked up to see the winged creature circling. It clicked and clacked, but it was like it couldn't see me. It must have sensed me, but it couldn't see me. And when I looked back down at myself, the reason was obvious. *I* could barely see me.

"Good afternoon, young man."

We turned to see an attendant approach. His grin was almost as big as Hazel's. He was dressed in overalls with the logo of the gas station on his pocket. "Fill her up?" he asked. "Check the oil? How 'bout those windows. Looks like they could use a little washing?"

"Uh, no," Jesse said. "I'm good."

"What say I look under that hood and check the ol' radiator? Past few days have been pretty hot, you know." I remember Mom and Dad talking about the good old days of full service gas stations, but this was ridiculous.

"Actually," Jesse said, "we just need directions."

"We?" the attendant asked.

Just to be safe, Jesse stepped between us so the attendant wouldn't freak by catching a glimpse of me (or not me). I took my cue, slipped out of the jacket, and eased myself back into the truck.

"What I mean is," Jesse cleared his throat, "how do I get to the nearest hospital?"

"Just six blocks down the street and to your left. Big white building. Can't miss it."

"Thanks." Jesse turned and climbed back into the truck.

"No problem. Hey, how 'bout those tires, want me to check the air?"

"No, but thanks."

"You betcha. Stop in again, anytime."

Jesse nodded. He dropped the truck into gear and we leaped forward, bouncing over the curb and back into

Honk! Honk!
CRAAAAAASH
tinkle tinkle tinkle

the street.

Glancing to where I was, or where he hoped I was, Jesse did his best to keep me calm. "Just hang in there, Jen. We'll get this all taken care of. Just don't go away."

"Go away?" I said. "Where would I go?" But even as I spoke I could tell my voice had nearly disappeared.

Chapter Thirteen

A FAMILY FEUD

J
A
K
E

"Jake . . . you hear . . . ?"

I woke up coughing and gagging, which is just the sort of thing a person does when he's lying facedown in goopy mud.

"Ja . . . can you . . . me?"

Even though the voice was breaking up, I was pretty sure I recognized it. "Gita?" I sputtered as I sat up in the muddy water. "Is that you?"

" . . . not hear . . . but . . ."

I blinked, shivering at the cold. "Gita? I can't understand you. Say again."

"... must ... now, before ..."

"Gita?" I strained to listen but if there was a voice it stopped. "Gita?"

Nothing.

My head ached like someone had bashed it with a hammer—or at least with a very drunk man flying off a very big man while holding a very hard rock. But when I raised my hand to rub it, I noticed my hand was all vapory. I shut my eyes, trying to clear my vision. But when I reopened them, I looked just as misty, like I was barely there. *Wow,* I thought, *I must have got hit in the head a lot harder than I thought.*

I struggled to my hands and knees and looked around. I was still at the top of the hill. But the party was definitely over. Oh, there were three or four folks sprawled out on benches and tables, another two or three lying in the mud. But since they were all passed out, it was safe to say the "good times" had come and gone.

To my right I heard a bunch of gruntings and squealings. I squinted through the early morning darkness and saw what looked like a heard of wild boars. I remember that on the National Geographic Channel (the only thing Dad watched when he was at home) wild boars were definitely something to avoid—especially the ones with giant tusks growing out of their mouths. Unfortunately, the goat they were gnawing on must have missed that particular episode. (**Note to Self:** Along with deer antlers and bull horns, avoid wild boar tusks.)

I also heard what sounded like voices coming from a hut at the bottom of the hill. They sounded like they might belong to Ham and his wife, but I couldn't be sure. I *was* sure that the hut was filled with light. I was also sure that light meant fire and fire meant heat. Something I could definitely use.

So, thanks to my great athletic ability, I was able to rise to my feet. Thanks to my pounding head, I dropped back to my knees. That's about the time I felt the ground begin to shake. At first I thought it was my imagination until I looked down and saw the ripples in the water growing bigger and bigger. Unless I was in a remake of *Jurassic Park*, I knew it could only be one thing:

Earthquake!

It was just like being back in California but without all the falling buildings and collapsing freeways. And with it, right on cue, came rain. And we're not talking a little. It was like the whole sky opened up. Big time. No problem for me, but it really shook up my little boar buddies. Which explains their shrieks and squeals and their not-so-little feet starting a not-so-little stampede.

Directly toward me!

Of course I remembered they were only super holographic images, but I also remembered how real those super holographic images felt when exposed to my super sensitive-to-death body. This would explain my leaping up and, despite my pounding head, running as fast as I could. Unfortunately, fast may not be fast enough when your feet are

squish-ing, *slurp*-ing,
and
suck-ing

through ankle-deep mud. And it's definitely not fast enough when those not-so-little boar feet that are coming after you don't seem to have that problem.

This, of course, would explain screaming my lungs out. "HELLLLLLP!" Unfortunately, the other thing about super holographic images is they can't exactly hear you. Not that it mattered.

What *did* matter was when I wasn't

squish-ing, *slurp*-ing,
and
suck-ing

I was

slipp-ing, *fall*-ing,
and
splash-ing

face-first back into the mud. The good news was I no longer screamed my lungs out. The bad news was you can't scream your lungs out when your mouth is full of mud.

I threw a look over my shoulder at the boars. They were gaining fast.

I leaped to my feet, *slip*-ped, fell, and *splash*-ed back down.

But this time I was close enough to the edge of the hill to start crawling on my hands and knees. The mud made me look like a chocolate covered peanut, and for once in my life I was glad no one was around to post my photo on Facebook.

Then, just as the animals arrived to insert their sharp

little hooves into my soft little body, I threw myself over the edge and slid down the hill.

Of course the boars were smart enough to stop so they didn't have the opportunity to hit every

SLAM . . . BAM

. . . man, that's going to leave a bruise

rock along the way. And, of course they missed every sharp and pointed

POKE . . . PROD . . . CUT

. . . so this is what open heart surgery feels like

stick along the way.

It was quite a ride. But as we know, all good things must come to an end. And for me that end involved

SLAMM-ing

through the door of the hut and coming to rest just a few feet from the table where Ham and his wife, Phelmona, were arguing with another couple.

The earthquake was over and I thought about standing up. But since I was getting a little tired of falling down and dealing with all those sound effects (you think it's a bother reading them, try living them), I decided to just lie there and eavesdrop . . . which was pretty easy to do since they were shouting pretty loud.

"See," Phelmona was saying, "the shaking of the earth, the pouring of the rain, they are all signs from the God of Noah. Please, brother, it is proof that what we are saying is true!"

Her brother, a tall dude who could have played for the L.A. Lakers if he was just a few thousand years younger, shook his head.

But Phelmona wouldn't let it go. She was real emotional and pressed in even more. "And the animals, you see them. They are coming from every direction."

Without answering, he reached across the table for a loaf of bread.

"Why do you not believe us?" Ham asked.

Her brother turned to him. "I mean no disrespect to you or to your family. But your father, he is . . ." He searched for the words.

"I know," Ham sighed. "My father is seen as the village fool."

Ripping off a chunk of bread, the man offered it to Ham, then to Phelmona. When they refused, he shrugged and stuffed it into his mouth. "First he claims that he has heard God speak directly to him. Then he says he has been commanded to build a giant boat because this God of his will flood the entire earth with water and destroy everything."

Ham nodded, staring down at the table a little embarrassed.

"Except for two of every kind of animal," Phelmona said. "They will survive because somehow they will know to enter the ark."

Her brother chuckled and Ham sighed. Phelmona wasn't exactly helping their case.

She continued. "Those who enter the ark will live. And those who don't . . ."

Her brother finished. "Will be swept away and forever destroyed."

"Exactly."

Ham shifted uncomfortably.

The big man looked at his sister. "And that doesn't sound, oh, I don't know, just a little crazy?"

"I suppose—maybe a little."

He tore off another piece of bread. "Maybe *a lot*."

Silence stole over the conversation. There was only the sound of rain on the thatched roof, and the fading squeals of the wild boars (who probably had the good sense to get out of the rain or at least find an ark).

At last the brother's wife spoke up. She was pretty, and like every other woman in the village, she was dressed scantily enough to prove it. "If this God of yours is so loving, why would He do such a thing to us?"

Ham stared at his hands a moment before answering. "Because He says . . ." he cleared his throat and tried again. "Because my father says it is God's judgment. People have grown so evil they no longer care what is right or wrong. They care only for what gives them pleasure."

"And for that he would destroy the entire world?" the woman asked. "With no possible way of survival?"

"But He has provided a way," Phelmona said. "At least for us. And maybe for you. If you choose to change your ways and enter the ark, perhaps you will also be saved."

The brother smiled and spread out his arms to include the hut. "And you would have me leave all of this behind? At the words of a madman, I am to simply walk away and leave our beautiful home?" I glanced around the hut. The guy barely had furniture, let alone an Xbox or a big-screen TV. Still, I knew what he meant.

His wife turned to Ham. "Did you not say this God would only save your brother, your wives, and your parents?"

"That is true," Ham agreed.

"But perhaps He is wrong," Phelmona said. "If others come on board, perhaps they will be saved too."

Her brother paused a moment, then tore off a final piece of bread. "I am sorry to disappoint you, little sister, but I do not like your God or His ways. Nor will I be foolish enough to believe them."

"My brother . . ." Phelmona reached out to him.

He gently took her hands and shook his head.

Phelmona could only stare at him, tears forming in her eyes. It was obvious he'd made up his mind. She looked across the table to his wife who also nodded. Finally she lowered her eyes. Tears came faster now, as they fell from her face and splattered onto the rough wooden table.

Chapter Fourteen

GOING . . . GOING . . . GONE

J
E
N
N
I
F
E
R

"Don't go, Jen. Hang on, we can do this." Jesse looked over to where I sat. If he couldn't see me, he didn't let on. But we both knew the terrible truth . . . if I was this far gone, it meant Dad was that much closer to dying.

I tried my best to encourage him. "I'm okay, but hurry!" He leaned forward to hear and I shouted at the top of my lungs. "HURRY!"

Before he could answer, a chill filled the truck. I couldn't figure it out. The windows were up. There was no wind blowing through me. So why on earth was—And then I heard it, that awful chortle, the clicking and clacking of the winged creature.

It had entered the back of the truck!

I stiffened as the sound grew closer. It was just a couple feet from my left ear. Slowly, and ever so silently, I turned. There it was, poking its shadow head through the seat between Jesse and me. Its red eye reflected everything on my side of the truck . . . everything but me.

I was totally invisible.

Its nostrils flared, sniffing the air like it was smelling. It tilted its head to one side, then the other, searching. It knew I was there, it just couldn't tell where. I held my breath so it couldn't hear me breathing. Why it didn't hear the hammering of my heart was beyond me.

I spotted the hospital just like the gas station attendant said. I wanted to tell Jesse, but I didn't. I wanted to turn my head for a better look, but I wouldn't. Luckily, Jesse saw it. "Here we go," he said, as he took a hard left into the emergency entrance.

The creature, who was still looking, blew out a breath in frustration. Then, to my horror, it turned its head so that it passed directly through me. Not toward me, not to me . . . but *through* me. That awful snout, the head, those glowing eyes, they were all inside me, passing through my neck and chest. Even if I wanted to scream, I couldn't. I was too paralyzed with fear.

Jesse skidded to a stop in front of the entrance and the creature turned its head back out of me to take a look.

"Okay!" Jesse reached for the door and opened it. "You stay here and I'll see what I can do, all right?"

There was no way I was answering him and there was no way I was staying inside the truck; not with that thing. Even though it went against everything I hated, I took a deep, silent breath, gritted my teeth and, scooted across the seat . . . right through the creature. The thing shook its head and snorted, like it felt something but couldn't tell what.

I climbed out as Jesse closed the door . . . right through me. It felt like a little puff of air, nothing more.

We raced through the parking lot. I stayed as close to Jesse as possible so he would block the wind. It was freezing cold, but I didn't care. I threw a look back to the truck. The winged creature was rising through the roof, cocking its head this way and that, still searching.

We entered the lobby and ran to the information desk. Some sweet old lady in a neatly pressed uniform told us Dad's room number. It was on the third floor. We took the elevator up and waited not-so-patiently for the doors to open. (I probably could have passed right through them, but I didn't feel like showing off.) We raced down the hallway and I noticed the walls were beginning to fade. So were the sounds. At least for me. Of course. If I quit existing how could I experience anything else that existed? How could I experience anything at all?

When we found Dad's room, Grandma Mackenzie was already there along with a doctor and a nurse. Dad was lying in the bed, his little body totally still.

"Excuse me," Jesse said as we barged in. "Excuse me."

Grandma Mackenzie turned to him. Her red, puffy eyes widened. "That's him!" she cried. "The boy whose sister chased Billy into the street!"

Jesse nodded. "Right. I know you won't believe this, but—"

"I'll have to ask you to leave," the doctor said.

"No, you don't understand."

"Where is she?" Grandma Mackenzie said. "Where is your sister?"

Jesse held his ground. "You don't understand. Let me explain."

The doctor stepped forward. "We have a very sick patient here, and—"

"I know, I know. But I think I can help." Of course, Jesse was bluffing. He had no idea how to help.

Without answering, the doctor turned to the nurse. "Lisa, will you call security, please?"

"Yes, Doctor." The nurse stepped out of the room while managing to—

"No, look out!"

—walk right through me.

Jesse moved closer to the bed. "I'm telling you, I can help."

"You dreadful boy." Grandma Mackenzie dabbed her eyes with a handkerchief. Her voice broke and she began to sob. "My baby's brain is swelling and there's nothing anyone can do."

The doctor rested an understanding hand on her shoulder. "Our best hope is to wait . . . and pray."

She nodded and continued to cry.

"Wait a minute," Jesse said. "His brain is swelling?"

The doctor barely answered with a nod.

"Well then . . ." he started getting excited. "I saw something like this in an old *ER* rerun."

They both ignored him.

"If his brain is swelling it's going to get all bruised and damaged by pushing against the skull, right?

More ignoring

But that didn't stop Jesse. "So why don't you remove a piece of the skull, you know, so it can swell without getting hurt. Then, when the swelling goes down, just replace that part of the skull."

The doctor seemed to hear. He hesitated then shook his head and frowned.

"Why not?"

"It's never been done before."

"It will be," Jesse insisted. "All the time in prime time and reruns."

"You awful child," Grandma Mackenzie turned and started toward him. "Get out!"

Jesse stepped back as she kept coming at him.

"Get out! Get out!" She finally drove us from the room.

"It'll work," Jesse shouted past her to the doctor. "I promise! It was on TV so it's gotta—"

She shut the door in his face.

My heart sank. There was nothing more we could do. It was over. Jesse knew it too. I wanted to say something. Even though he couldn't hear me and even though we failed, I wanted to tell him how much I appreciated his help. So, more to myself than to him, I said, "Thank you, Jesse. Thanks."

He looked up startled. "What?"

I blinked, surprised he heard.

"Jenny, is that you?"

"Yeah," I said, my voice growing louder by the second. "I'm right here."

He turned, looking until he spotted me. Then he broke into that heart-stopping grin of his.

"What's going on?" I asked.

"You're coming back," he said. "Loud and clear."

I looked down at my hands then my body. He was right. They were completely visible and getting more solid by the second. "But . . . how's that possible?" My voice was totally normal.

Jesse turned back to the closed door. "He must have heard. He thought it was crazy, but the doctor must have heard. And since it was like your dad's only chance—"

"He going to try the procedure?" I said.

"Yes!" Jesse turned back to me, grinning even bigger "He's going to try the procedure and your dad's going to live."

"Jesse!" I couldn't believe it. "You did it!"

He broke out laughing and took both of my hands. "I can see you, plain as day!" He threw his arms around me. "I was so scared, Jen. I thought I was going to lose you!"

The hug shocked him as much as me. But it was true, I was back. And if I needed any more proof, all I had to do was feel my ears turning beat red and feel the herd of butterflies doing backflips in my stomach. But before I could enjoy the moment, let alone write any love poems or decide how many children we'd have once we got married and lived happily ever after, he pulled away from me and said, "Do you still have that time beam generator?"

"Yes." I felt for it inside my coat pocket and pulled it out.

"Great." He reached into his own jacket and pulled out the dimensional folder. "Let's get out of here before we do any more damage."

"You there!"

We spun around to see the nurse appear with a security guard on one side and the thin, bald policeman who'd been questioning me on the other.

Jesse turned to me and said, "Now what?"

I spotted the stairway door to our right and had our answer.

Chapter Fifteen

AND AWAY WE GO . . . AGAIN

J
E
N
N
I
F
E
R

Even though running down the stairs to avoid getting thrown in jail was not my favorite pastime, it was nice to have my body back. We arrived at the main floor and were about to open the lobby door when Jesse brought us to a stop.

"Wait a minute," he said. "We came back in time to get your dad?"

"Right."

"To bring him to our century?"

"Right."

"So we still have to zap him with your time bean generator, right?"

I paused then shook my head. "Wrong."

"Wrong?"

"Right."

"So I'm wrong saying we *don't* have to bring him back to our century?"

"Not, that's wrong, you're right."

"I'm right about being wrong?"

"Right?"

Jesse gave me a look. "Want to start over?"

I took a quick breath and explained. "We need to bring Dad back to our century. But if we bring him back to our century, who will be left in this one?"

Jesse opened his mouth then closed it realizing he had no answer. Neither did I.

I sighed wearily, "Don't you just hate time travel?"

He nodded and reached for the door. But he'd barely opened it before he stopped.

"What's wrong?"

He pulled back to let me see. The lobby was swarming with police. Ever so gently, he closed the door.

"What do we do?" I asked.

Before he could answer, we heard commotion on the stairs a couple stories above us.

Jesse set his dimensional folder on the floor. "Set your time generator," he whispered.

"To what?"

"Back home. We gotta get out of here."

I nodded and adjusted the dials. "What about Dad?"

"Hold it right there, kids."

We looked up to see the skinny cop coming down the steps. He was one flight away.

Jesse snapped on the dimensional folder and the lights began flashing. I clicked on the standby switch. The generator started **HUMMM**-ing and the lenses began spinning.

The policeman rounded the last flight of stairs. "Play time's over, kids."

"Not quite," Jesse whispered as we stepped onto the dimensional folder. The lights flashed faster as I pointed the time generator at us and

CRACKLE

FLASH

As the flash faded I saw the stars shooting past me again . . . just like old times.

"Jen?" Jesse was beside me. "We're folding dimensions again?"

I nodded. Although it still made me uneasy, I loved this first part. I held my breath and listened as the singing began, soft and lovely. I glanced to Jesse. He was enjoying it too. It was so beautiful the way the voices folded and blended into each other. Once again I felt the softness as the feathers brushed against my face, against my whole body, embracing and tenderly holding me. The music kept swelling until the light began to soak into me. I held out my hands, marveling at the way my fingers and palms started to glow, filling me with more and more of the light, the music, the voices. I closed my eyes and let it wash through me.

"Jen." Jesse's voice sounded far away. "Jen . . ."

I opened my eyes and saw that once again he was lower than me. While I seemed to be rising faster with the light in and around me growing brighter, it looked like he'd stopped moving altogether.

"Jen!"

We were about a hundred feet apart when I again saw the red light flickering through him as he tried to rise higher. He cried out in pain as tried again, then again, but with no success. I wanted to slow down, to go back and help. But I wasn't sure how. And then, just like before, the singing turned to English:

"Greetings, Daughter of the King."

There was that phrase again.

"Jen!"

My friend, I thought. *Why have you stopped my friend?*

"He has stopped himself."

I don't understand.

"For his protection he may come no further."

You said that before. But why can I rise and he can't? It doesn't seem fair.

"It is what you have chosen."

I frowned.

"You have chosen the Pure to make you pure."

The Pure. What is the Pure?

"Not what, Who."

I paused, trying to put it together. *God? Do you mean the Pure is God?*

"The One who suffered your impurities to make you pure."

But I'm not pure.

"You are pure because He declared you Pure."

It sounded strangely familiar. Maybe I understood, maybe I didn't. But it was worth taking a guess. *Jesus?* I asked. *Are you talking about Jesus?*

"The Pure has many names."

I looked back down to Jesse who was growing smaller by the minute. *And my friend—*

"—has not yet chosen the Pure."

Not yet? I thought. *But he can, right? I mean He can choose the Pure too. Choose the Pure to make him pure?*

"Life is full of choices."

The light around me began rippling. Before I knew it, some sort of diagram with pictures floated below me. Only the pictures were moving like they were alive, like scenes from a bunch of 3D movies. And, this was the cool part, they were all scenes of my life—starting way back from when I was just a baby. Each scene was connected with a vibrating beam of green light. Most of the time the beam led to another scene. But sometimes it led to a totally white area with no scene at all, before it continued to the next scene, and the next, and so on. It was amazing. Like I could look down and see my entire life.

Wait a minute. If I could to see my entire life, did that mean it was over, that I was dead?

The thought had barely formed before the song answered, "No. You are merely seeing life from a higher dimension."

I swallowed. *From . . . heaven?*

"Heaven is much higher. From here you only see your choices."

I looked back down. Not far away was a scene where I was four or five years old. Jake was tormenting me at the breakfast table. I'd just picked up a heavy milk glass and was about to throw it at him when the scene stopped and the beam of light connected it to another scene. But the new one was entirely white. Another beam connected that white scene to the next scene where I sat in a hospital ER room bawling my eyes out as Jake was next door getting stitches.

I looked down the row of scenes and saw another where I was seven. My friends, Julie and Savannah, were daring me to steal a Snickers bar from the candy rack at our local Target. At first I refused, but gradually I caved in. I continued watching as I finally reached for the candy bar. But just before I took it, the scene stopped and was connected to another one that was completely white.

And on and on it went like that, one scene after another. Most of the times regular scenes were connected to regular scenes, but sometimes they were connected to the white ones.

What's going on? I thought.

There was only singing.

I tried again. *What are those white scenes? The ones where I did bad stuff?*

"They no longer exist."

What do you mean? I remember some of them perfectly.

"The Pure doesn't. The Pure declared you pure so you are pure."

You mean all of those things are . . . forgotten?

"The Pure declares you pure so you are pure."

I continued to stare as the song changed its melody. "You must see your brother."

Jake?

"You must see."

Is there something wrong?

There was no answer. Only the blurring of my life images as they rippled and became Jake's.

Chapter Sixteen

ALMOST FAREWELL

J
A
K
E

We'd barely stepped outside Phelmona's brother's hut when the earth started shaking again. Big time. So big that between the shaking, rain, and mud, I went back to my favorite hobby of

slipp-ing, *fall*-ing
and
splash-ing.

"What's happening?" Phelmona cried grabbing Ham so she wouldn't fall.

He shouted back, "It is God's anger!"

Of course I wanted to explain that it was just an earthquake and had nothing to do with God's anger. I mean if that were the case, God would really be upset with California and all the stuff that . . . Hm, wait a minute, let me get back to you on that. Anyway, the point is this earthquake was super-strong, super-long and, just to keep things interesting, there was major lightning and majorer (is that a word?) thunder.

"Phelmona!" a voice shouted. "Ham! Over here!"

Not far away, in the doorway of another hut, stood Enthal, the girl who was so helpless that I'd tried to rescue her earlier.

"Inside!" she yelled. "Quickly!"

They didn't have to be told twice. And once I staggered to my feet, *slipp*-ing, *fall*-ing and *splash*-ing for old time's sake, neither did I. We entered the tiny hut and after the usual hugs and terrified cries of, "WHAT'S GOING ON? WE'RE ALL GOING TO DIE!" the quake finally settled down and the earth stopped shaking.

But not Ham, Phelmona, and Enthal. There were also two whimpering puppies, brown and black, who rated about an 11 on the cute scale. They were huddled in the corner of the room doing their own brand of shaking.

"Cousin, is it true?" Enthal's eyes were wide with fear. Without that stupid glazed look of being drunk, they were all the more beautiful and innocent. "Is your God really going to destroy the world?"

Phelmona took her hands and nodded just as another flash of lightning lit up the sky, followed by a deafening clap of thunder.

Enthal shivered. "I am so afraid."

"Then come with us," Phelmona said.

The girl hesitated. "Is that possible?" She turned to Ham.

He answered. "The Lord promised to save only our family—"

"But if you come on board with us, perhaps," Phelmona cleared her voice nervously, "perhaps He will change His mind."

Enthal threw a cautious look to what must have been the bedroom. "But what of Naalamachelruha? What would he think?"

"It doesn't matter what anybody thinks," Ham said.

Phelmona added, "We heard how he treated you last night."

The girl glanced down. "Then you also heard how I'd been so . . . so . . ."

"Drunk?" Phelmona asked gently.

She nodded.

"That was last night," Ham said. "Today is a new day. Turn to God. He will give you the strength not to do such things again.

Lightning flashed again, brighter. The thunder boomed louder. And the puppies in the corner whimpered and huddled together even closer.

"But," Enthal said, "it wasn't just me. Everyone was drinking, they were all drunk."

"And that makes it right?" Ham said.

Phelmona added, "If everybody does wrong, why must you?"

"Because . . ." She searched for the words. "Because . . ."

"Dear cousin, you must stop worrying what others think. There is only One whose opinion matters." More lightning. So close we could hear it sizzle through the air and the thunder explode above our heads. "He is the only one who can save you."

The girl looked from Phelmona to Ham, then back to Phelmona. I knew she was just a projected image, but that didn't stop me from feeling sorry for her and wanting to help. Maybe it was those eyes, I don't know, but she was really getting to me. Before I could stop myself I stepped toward her and said, "The world's going to end! Don't you get it? God's not messing around."

Of course no one heard me and Ham continued. "Following God is the only way.

Enthal hesitated. "Does anybody else in the village believe what you say? Your brother, any of our cousins?"

Phelmona's eyes filled with sadness and Ham answered for her. "No, nobody."

Enthal stared at the ground thinking, then she raised her chin. "Then neither do I."

I practically shouted, "What are you talking about? Stop following the crowd and be your own person!"

"Jake . . ." It was Gita's voice again. " . . . can you . . . me? Jake . . ."

"Not now, Gita!" I wasn't sure she could hear. I really didn't care. Somebody had to get through to this girl.

The rain turned to hail, pounding the roof like a thousand tap dancers gone crazy.

Ham shouted over the noise. "There isn't much time. We must hurry!"

Enthal looked back down and shook her head. "I am sorry."

"Are you nuts?" I yelled. "Of course you—"

The tree outside exploded with lightning and burst into flames.

Ham took his wife's arm. "We must go."

But Phelmona would not budge. She turned to Enthal, tears filling her eyes. "Please, cousin. Turn to God. Change your ways."

Enthal had also started to cry. She shook her head and tried to answer, but the words wouldn't come. I couldn't believe it. There had to be some way to make her see reason. Some way to stop her from following the herd.

"Now, Phelmona!" Ham shouted. "We must go now!"

The two women fell into each others arms crying as the light from the burning tree flickered through the doorway across their faces.

"Phelmona!"

They kissed each other again and again until Ham finally succeeded in pulling his wife away. Then he and Phelmona turned and headed out into the storm.

Suddenly Enthal called after her. "Cousin!"

Phelmona stopped and turned. As she did, Enthal disappeared from the doorway. A moment later she returned and ran out into the storm. She held the two shivering puppies in her arms. "Will you take these?"

Phelmona turned to her husband who didn't look happy.

"Please," Enthal begged, "they are like my children. Please, save them?"

Finally, Phelmona reached out and took the puppies. They squirmed and wiggled as she did her best to protect them from the rain.

Enthal watched, biting her lip. Finally she spoke. "Good-bye, cousin."

Phelmona looked at her one last time, then nodded and turned, unable to take anymore. With Ham leading the way, the couple quickly disappeared into the storm.

Enthal stood there, watching. Only the light from the burning tree lit her face, showing the tears mixed with rain.

I was pretty choked up too. There had to be some way to make her see. Yeah, she had her problems, but down deep inside you could tell she was a good person and that she wanted to go.

Finally, she turned and brushed past me into the hut. It was then I knew exactly what I had to do. I'd stay behind. Not long. Just enough to convince her. I knew she couldn't see or hear me, but some way, some how I had to make her understand.

Chapter Seventeen

A BRIEF LAYOVER

J
E
N
N
I
F
E
R

What happened?

I'd been staring down at the scenes of my brother's life until they suddenly stopped. No connecting beams of light. Nothing.

Why did it end? I thought. *Why are there no more scenes?*

The voices kept singing.

Excuse me! Why did the scenes stop?

"There are no more."

No more scenes? Why not?

"It is his choice."

Despite the beautiful singing and light and everything, a cold dread swept over me. As it did, the sensation of rising slowly came to a stop. *Why?* I thought. *What's his choice?*

"There are no more scenes."

You said that, but why? Why are there no more scenes? I felt myself beginning to fall. *Is he going to die? Is that what you're saying? There are no more scenes because he has no more life?* I fell faster. It wasn't scary or anything, more like being in a fast elevator.

"Life is full of choices."

Are you saying he's going to die because that's what he wants?

The lyrics repeated, "Life is full of choices."

But he doesn't know! He doesn't know the danger he's in!

"It will be his choice."

No! Someone's got to warn him!

"Jen?"

I looked down and saw I was falling toward Jesse. "We've got to warn him!" I shouted.

"What? Warn who? What's going on?"

I was still picking up speed. "Reach out and grab my hands!"

He stretched out his arms. "What's happening?"

I was nearly on top of him. "Jake's still in the Machine. He won't come out. Grab me!"

We stretched out our hands to catch each other. I was going so fast the force nearly broke our grip. Nearly.

Somehow we hung on. But instead of Jesse stopping me from falling, I pulled him down with me.

Now we were both falling.

"We've got to warn him," I shouted. "He's at the bottom of a hill, in a small hut."

"What about your dad?"

I nodded, my thoughts spinning. "I know, I know. We've got to save him too." I looked down and saw we were approaching the red, flickering light. "Close your eyes," I shouted. "This is the part we close our eyes."

"Got it," he said.

I closed my eyes as the light, the singing, and the sensation of feathers faded into a crimson red . . . and the creepy clicking and clackings of those winged creatures. As always it was terrifying, but I kept my eyes closed.

The good news was the color and sounds also faded.

The bad news was, Jesse wasn't so great at following instructions.

"Jen . . ."

"We're almost there," I said.

"Jen, you might want to see this."

"Are your eyes open?"

"You better take a look."

Against my judgment, I opened my eyes. The stars were shooting past just like they always did at the beginning of our trips. Nothing unusual there. What was unusual was to see a boy and girl about our age flying up at us. Actually, they were *exactly* our age. And they looked *exactly* like us. The reason was simple.

"They're us!" I cried.

And I was right. Same clothes, same hair, same every-thing. Only this Jesse and Jennifer were doing it the right way. They were both keeping their eyes shut.

"Cute couple," Jesse chuckled.

I shot him a look.

"So," he said, "if they're just starting their trip and we're just finishing ours . . ."

I looked at him, waiting for more.

"Could that be like us when we first started?"

I scowled. "You mean are we . . . are we passing our-selves in time?"

He shrugged. "It's a thought."

And a pretty good one. But right now there were other worries. We were about fifty feet from them, and with their rising and our falling it looked like we were about to have a major, head-on collision.

"Look out!" Jesse shouted. "Get out of the way."

But they didn't hear.

I let go of his hands and started swinging my arms and kicking my legs like I was swimming.

"What are you doing?"

"I'm trying to get out of the way!"

It must have made sense because he joined in. Of course it would have made more sense if we'd made any progress. But every time we moved to the left, they drifted to the left. When we moved to the right, they drifted to the right. It was like we were magnets being drawn toward each other.

Now they were twenty feet away.

Make that ten.

Jesse braced himself for the collision. "This could hurt."

Five feet.

I covered my head with my arms.

And then . . .

Nothing. I mean we must have hit but I felt nothing. No jolt, no bump, not even a touch. And when I looked up to where they should be, no one was there. I turned to Jesse who was also looking up.

"Where'd they go?"

He shook his head. "I don't know. Unless, since they were us . . ." He hesitated.

"Go on."

"Since they were us, maybe they're . . . us."

I frowned.

So did he. Then with the slightest grin he repeated what I'd said earlier, "Don't you just hate time travel?"

In spite of myself, I had to grin back . . . just as the streaking stars around us faded and the sensation of moving came to an end. The lab tent wavered in front of us then appeared in plain sight as, once again, we were back in the lab standing on the dimensional folder.

I stepped off the platform to check the time on Robbie's computer. Less than an hour had passed.

Jesse joined me. "What are you thinking?"

"We've got to hurry and rescue my brother."

"What about your dad?"

"Right, right." I rubbed my head, trying to think.

"The Machine, it's pretty safe now?" Jesse asked.

"It's still got a few bugs, but yeah."

"Great, then give me the time beam generator."

I pulled it from my coat and stopped. "Why?"

"You go get your brother and I'll find your dad."

"But . . ." I looked back down at the dimensional folder platform. "Crossing dimensions—you saw how dangerous it was."

"Exactly. Which is why I should go."

It was a sweet idea but I shook my head. "It's safer if I go."

"Why?"

"You saw how you got stuck. I've made choices you haven't made."

"Choices? About what?"

"Long story." I reached for the computer keyboard and under LOCATION typed:

University of Washington

"Choices about what?"

"God and Jesus and stuff." I hit ENTER and the platform lights began flashing again.

"What are you doing?"

I looked down at the time beam generator, thought a moment, then set the date to:

April 1, 1971

"Jen?

"April Fool's day. That's the day my dad was arrested at the University of Washington for doing something stupid. Mom always used to tease him about it."

"So?"

"So I know he's a brainiac and I know he'll be there. Once he's done freaking out over me, he ought to be able to figure everything out."

I headed to the platform, its lights flashing faster and faster.

"What about me?"

"Save my brother." I stepped onto the platform. "He's in the Machine trying to save some girl before the flood. Get him out of there before it happens." I flipped the Standby switch on the generator and the lenses spun as it began to

HUMMM

Only then did it hit me how tricky and risky it all was. Jesse must have seen the fear on my face.

"Jenny!"

I took a breath and did my best imitation of a smile. "Wish me luck."

But thinking he still had to be my protector, he raced toward me.

I saw it coming and had a different idea. Not exactly better, but different. As he leaped onto the platform, I jabbed him hard in the gut with my elbow (see what I mean about not better?). When he doubled over, I nudged him off the platform and he sort of tumbled to the floor. (Make that *way* not better.)

As he looked up, those big baby blues filled with hurt and betrayal, I managed to croak out a, "Sorry," before pulling the trigger. The dimensional folder

CRACKLE-ed

The time beam generator

FLASH-ed

and I was gone.

Chapter Eighteen

BREAKTHROUGH

J
E
S
S
E

I raced through the camp hearing the thunder clap and rumble from the Machine. I rounded the last tent and saw all sorts of animals fenced off and kept away from the staging area. And there, in the very center of the area, sat the ark. It was surrounded by black, angry clouds and rain coming down so hard you could barely see it . . . except for the blinding flashes of lightning every few seconds.

Gita, Robbie, and that crazy Hazel girl with the chimpanzee were working on the control console. Well, Gita, Robbie, and Hazel were working. The chimp was busy sucking and chewing on the various tools lying around.

"Guys," I shouted, "have you found Jake yet?"

Robbie looked up. "Hey dude, where's your woman?"

"My what?"

"Your babe, your chick, your numero uno momma."

I took a stab at answering, grateful that Jen wasn't around to hear. "You mean Jennifer? Oh, she's, uh, she's fine."

"You guys weren't fooling with my time beam generator were you?"

"What? Why would you say that?" It wasn't exactly a lie, but it wasn't exactly the truth, either. Unfortunately, Robbie could tell the difference.

"Not cool, dude." He rose from the console. "Didn't I tell you to hold off and I'd get Dr. Mackenzie?"

"Well, yeah, but—"

"Time travel is definitely not for newbies."

I said nothing as he angrily headed for the tents.

Hazel gazed after him. "Isn't he fantastic?" she said. "There's absolutely nothing he can't do."

Neither Gita or I answered. And the chimp was busy pulling off strips of black electrician's tape, rolling them into little balls, and popping them into his mouth.

I looked back to the staging area and the storm raging inside. "Any news on Jake?"

Gita shook her head. "He is still in there." She wiped the sweat from her face. "We are attempting to contact him, but the electrical storm is interfering with our transmission."

"Why doesn't somebody just go in after him?"

"It's too dangerous," Hazel said. "We don't know where he is."

"The staging area isn't that big."

"Not from out here. But once you're inside it fools your senses into believing it goes on forever."

Maximilian coughed, spit up a wad of electrician's tape and gave the world's loudest and longest

BUUUURP . . .

I had to make my move. Jen said every second counted. But Gita and Hazel were directly between me and the staging area. I had to be subtle. To turn up the ol' charm; be smooth and nonchalant. So, sticking my hands into my pockets, I casually strolled past the console. Nobody paid attention except Maximilian, who eyed me suspiciously.

I added to my disguise by humming. It seemed to do the trick for everyone, except the pesky chimp who had started to frown.

I hummed louder.

He frowned harder, cocking his head one way, then the other.

Figuring he didn't like the song, I changed tunes and hummed something else.

He gave a snarl.

I gave a smile.

He gave a growl.

I picked up my pace.

He hoped off the console making little "Ooo-ooo-ahh-ahh-eee-eee" sounds then took off after me.

I took off away from him.

"Hey!" Hazel shouted. "Where do you think you're going? You can't go in there!"

But there was no turning around. I was twenty feet from the staging area and closing in fast. Unfortunately Maximilian was ten feet away from me and closing in faster.

"Do not proceed!" Gita shouted. "It is too dangerous!"

I was ten feet away.

Maximilian was five.

"Maxi, sweetie!" Hazel called. "Come back."

But Maxi Sweetie was as determined to catch me as I was determined to get inside. I reached the edge of the staging area just as a series of lightning flashes and thunder went off. I paused for the briefest second. Maximilian didn't. He tackled me hard. So hard we rolled across the dry, desert sand. Well, it had been dry, desert sand. Now it was a soggy, grassy field . . . with a giant ark right in front of us. And a powerful storm flashing and exploding all around us.

I broke from Maximilian's hold and staggered to my feet. "Uh-oh," I said.

He rose and looked at the storm. "Ooo-ooo," he said.

Peering into the rain was like looking into a shower running full force during a rainy day in the middle of Niagara Falls. I turned back to the control console. But it was nowhere in sight. Gita was right. My new world seemed to stretch on forever. The hills, the forests . . . **AND THE HUNDREDS OF WILD ANIMALS RACING TOWARD US!**

Sorry, didn't mean to yell. But you'd yell too if you saw every animal you could imagine—and some you couldn't— coming at you. And we're not talking a neat little line of animals walking two by two. We're talking about a mass of animals stampeding swarm by swarm!

Maximilian's wild beast nature kicked into gear. He screamed and waved his arms wildly. But screaming and waving your arms wildly doesn't do much to stop a charging hippo . . . or her mate. What did help was my ducking and weaving like we were playing a football game. But instead of a powerful quarterback on the field, I felt like a little mouse. Actually, a little flea on a little mouse. Actually a little mite on a little flea on a—well, you get the picture.

After the fortieth or so close call, I made it to a tiny little tree and managed to climb up it. Unfortunately Maximilian managed to grab my foot and climb up *me*. I didn't mind helping him out. Though it would have been best to check with the tree because it immediately began to

creeeeak

as it bent. It didn't bend far, just enough to freak out Maximilian

   . . . causing him to scamper up higher to my waist

   . . . causing the tree to

CREEEEAK

louder and lower

   . . . causing him to scream and crawl higher

   . . . causing me to scream louder

   . . . causing the tree to

CREEEEAK

lower until we were eye level to the stampede.

Well, not quite.

Since I'm not exactly Mr. Muscles and since Maximilian could stand to lose a few dozen pounds, my grip eventually slipped and we both

AUGH!
OOO-OOO-AHH-AHH-EEE-EEE!

fell.

The good news was it was onto the back of a zebra.

The bad news was the zebra was not picking up hitchhikers.

This would explain his kicking, jumping, and bucking. It would also explain our being thrown off of him and flying high through the air (without the luxury of an in-flight movie or complimentary soft drink).

But all good things must come to an end . . . even if it happened to be our lives.

Chapter Nineteen

ENCOUNTER

J
E
N
N
I
F
E
R

You'd think all this traveling through time and multiple dimensions would get to be old hat. But it wasn't. The streaming stars, the beautiful singing, the feathers brushing my skin, and that incredible light swirling around and soaking into me—how could that ever get old?

Then of course there were the words to the singing.

Soon I was able to understand them again. "What joy to see you, Daughter."

Thanks, I thought.

Eventually we traveled to the place where they began singing, "It is time to close your eyes."

Right. But of course I wasn't going to. I mean look what I almost missed the last time. Besides, I knew what was coming; the creepy winged creature. I wasn't looking forward to it, but I could handle it. I knew from experience. I had the authority.

Reading my mind, the lyrics sang, "Some things you are not ready to see."

I noticed my hands were already filling with the light and music. *Don't worry about me, I'll be okay.*

"Daughter." I heard a trace of concern in the voices. "You do not have the faith to endure what you see."

Faith?

"In His love. In His power."

If you're talking about God, I have faith He can do anything.

"But you do not believe." As the voices sang, the feathers brushed against my face, then over my eyes.

What are you doing?

"Protecting you."

Thanks, but no. I pushed away the feathers. They came back faster and thicker. *Come on, I want to see.* I pushed them away again and noticed the faintest trace of red filling the air around me. We were coming up to the scary part, but like I said, I knew I could handle it. The voices must have thought so too, cause they started to fade.

"Your fear is greater than your King."

Wait a minute, what's that supposed to mean?

They continued fading. "Your fear is greater than your Father.

"Follow the path, do not lose the light."

What?

"Follow the path."

I could barely hear them.

"Do not lose the light. Follow the . . ."

And then they were gone.

"Hello?"

There was no sound, no feelings of feathers, only the sensation of rising.

"Are you there? Hello?"

The silence was complete. I'd never heard anything so quiet. A shiver crawled across my shoulders. The light was redder and growing redder by the second. But that was okay. I had the authority. I'd used it several times already. Then, right on time, I heard the clicking and clacking. Faint at first, but quickly growing. The growling followed. All this as the red glow kept getting brighter and brighter until—

I sucked in my breath. The red wasn't just a color. It was eyes. I was looking into eyes! Thousands of them. Millions of them. The eyes of the winged creatures were crowding together staring at me! They surrounded every side, pressing in closer and closer. I tried to catch my breath, but could only manage a short, quick gasp.

"FOLLOW THE PATH!" The voices came back louder. I could tell they were yelling, but it was like they couldn't shout over my fear.

Everywhere I looked there were red glowing eyes. The

flickering I'd always thought was fire had actually been their blinking.

By now the clicking, clacking, and growling roared in my ears.

"FOLLOW THE PA . . ." The voices were gone. Even if they shouted I couldn't hear them.

I kept searching, trying to see past the eyes until—There! A flicker of light. I stretched my neck, tilted my head and—There it was again! A beam of green light like I'd seen the last time, the type connecting different scenes of my life. It was just below me, barely visible, but close enough to see . . . and follow.

I heard the creatures rustling their wings as they began shifting, trying to block my view. They lunged and jabbed their beaks like they were going to peck me but, oddly enough, they never touched me. I kept my eyes on that glowing beam of light and moved closer. Nothing would make me look away.

"Jenny?"

The voice came from my right. Only one word, but I instantly recognized it and turned. "Mom!"

"Jenny? Is that you?"

My heart pounded in excitement as I reached out past the heads and glowing eyes. I didn't know if they would attack or what, but that was my mom. To my surprise, the light coming from my hands forced them back. They screeched like they were afraid I was going to touch them. But as they pulled away, others filled their place. I waved my arms at them and they all dropped back. All right! I'd found a way to move through them.

"Mom?"

"Jenny!"

I shifted my weight toward her voice. I kept waving my arms and the things kept retreating. I began kicking my feet and moving my hands through the air like I was swimming. They screeched and clicked and growled, practically crawling on top of each other to get out of the way. Good. As long as I kept my arms out in front of me I was okay. They stayed two or three feet back, which was enough for me to keep moving toward her voice.

"Jennifer." She was a lot closer. "Jenny?"

And then I spotted her. "MOM!"

She was surrounded by the same winged creatures, dozens of them. But she had no light glowing inside to protect her. She was lying down, tears streaming from her eyes.

"Mom, are you okay?"

"Jenny. Dear Jenny."

I moved closer, feeling my throat tighten, my own eyes burning with tears. She'd died in a car crash over a year ago and now here she was. In the creepy red glow of their eyes she was lying in bed. No. No, that wasn't a bed. It was a coffin. She was in a coffin like the very last time I saw her. Her hair was neatly brushed, her hands folded over her chest. But now she was alive! I could see her breathing, I could see her eyes blinking. She didn't seem able to move, but she was *definitely* alive.

I heard the creatures closing in behind me, but what did I care. As long as I kept my hands stretched out, the things in front of me kept pulling back.

"Mom," I was just a few feet from her. "Where are we? This can't be heaven."

"No, sweetheart." She began to sob. "I never made it to heaven."

"What?"

"I was not good enough."

"But . . ." I was practically beside her. "You're the best person I've ever known."

"I was not good enough." As she spoke she didn't look at me. She continued staring straight ahead like she was paralyzed or something. "My sins were too many."

"But you always said Jesus forgave us—that all we had to do was ask."

She tried to answer but only sobbed louder. At last I arrived. The glow of the red light sparkled and reflected in her tears. Since she couldn't move her hands, I reached out to gently brush the tears away. But as soon as the light from my fingers touched her skin, her body convulsed. She threw back her head and howled in pain.

I yanked my hand away. "I'm sorry!" I cried. "What did I do?"

She couldn't answer. Her whole body was twisting and writhing in pain.

"Mom!"

There was a terrible cracking sound. I watched in horror as black, leathery wings sprouted from her shoulders. Her skin shimmered as shiny, snake-like scales began covering it. Her face narrowed and became birdlike as her nose and mouth grew into a beak. Her eyes grew larger and larger then finally began glowing that awful red.

I screamed and spun around, but the beaks and eyes of the other creatures were a solid wall behind me. And the path, the beam of light, where was it? I waved my arms.

The creatures parted but I saw nothing before they closed back in. I waved again and they pulled back. But again there was no light.

I turned, looking every direction, but I'd moved too far from the path. I'd lost it. And there were too many creatures in the way to see past them. Even though they couldn't touch me, they kept trying to direct me, closing in on one side and opening up a way on the other. Instinctively I followed until, NO! I had to find the light. The path was all that mattered. That and my mother. But when I turned back to look, she was completely gone . . . or completely changed, I couldn't tell her from any of the others.

Hundreds of them, thousands of them flooded in from every direction, pushing in tighter and tighter, closer and closer. Their clicking and growling filled my head. I covered my ears trying to think. That's when the first struck—a razor-sharp beak that pecked the back of my bare arm. I screamed and waved my hand, but even as it pulled away another rushed in, pecking away. And then another. And another. They shrieked in obvious pain from touching the light inside me, but it didn't matter. More beaks came. They went for my face. When I covered it, they attacked my bare hands. I screamed as they began tearing at my clothes, ripping my shirt, my pants, cutting through to my legs.

I was surrounded. No place to go. No place to hide when suddenly, Gita's words came to mind. *You are the one with the power.*

Was it still true? I knew I could beat one of them, but here there were so many.

You are the one with the power.
But—
If you put your faith in Jesus . . .
I took a ragged breath.
You have the authority.
I took another breath. And then I screamed, "Leave me alone!"
They may have let up, but only slightly.
If you put your faith in Jesus, you have the authority.
"In the name of Jesus!" I shouted.
They slowed.
"In the name of Jesus Christ I demand you leave!"
They came to a stop.
"Now!"
They clicked and cackled.
"NOW! LEAVE NOW!"
Suddenly, light exploded. Blinding white, all around. I pulled my hands from my face and stole a peak. There was no red. The air was completely clear. Well, not completely, but enough to see the green beam of light off in the distance. I kicked my feet and swam toward it.
The creatures closed back in. One started diving toward me.
"No!" I shouted. "In the name of Christ!"
It screeched and veered off.
The light was below me. Two more of them rushed in.
"No!" I shouted. "I forbid it!"
They screamed and flew off until finally, *finally*, I arrived and hovered over the beam of light. I began following it. As I did, the surrounding light grew whiter and brighter. And with it, the singing:

"Follow the path."

You're back, I thought.

"*You* are back," the voices sang.

What happened, what was that all about?

"Your fears were greater than your King."

So, no way was that Mom?

"She is with your King, just as He promised."

Then why—

"You chose to believe your fears instead of His truth."

I took another deep breath. I was beginning to understand. I believed more in my fears than in the King. So, at least in my head, my fears were greater than my King. As I thought this over I heard other voices, but not singing. They were more like a chant, and not nearly as beautiful.

As they grew louder, the light shifted around me. Other images shimmered and appeared until I realized I was standing in the middle of a street. It was raining and all around me there were long-haired, college kids. Lots of them carried signs saying things like, "Make Love Not War" and "Give Peace a Chance."

Up ahead, some woman with stringy, neon-red hair was shouting into a blow horn, "What do we want?"

The crowd around me shouted back, "Peace!"

"When do we want it?" she shouted.

"Now!"

We were scrunched together pretty tight so as the crowd moved forward, I moved with them.

It was great to be back home. Well, at least back in our three dimensions. I pulled out the time beam generator and checked the year. It still read, *1971*. Great. Except for that little field trip through who knew what, I was back on track.

"What do we want?"

"Peace!"

I looked around, guessing I was in the middle of some sort of war protest like we'd seen in history class.

"When do we want it?"

"Now!"

And if you couldn't tell by all the bearded hippies around me, you could tell by the line of policemen just ahead—the ones tapping their billy clubs into the palm of their hands, waiting for us to arrive.

Chapter Twenty

CONTACT

**J
E
N
N
I
F
E
R**

"What do we want?"

"Peace!"

"When do we want it?"

"Now!"

The stringy-haired redhead kept screaming through her blow horn and the crowd kept shouting back as we marched closer and closer to the police who weren't screaming or shouting . . . just tapping their billy clubs and looking anything but happy.

There were a hundred of us jammed together in the street so tight I could barely move. I could only go where they went which, at the moment, looked like trouble. It was like I was in one those old-fashioned photos where all the flower children were in their hippie clothes, hippie hair, hippie beards (and, for the record, hippie lack of mouth-wash and showers). But there was one fellow four or five people over who was dressed differently. Talk about a fish out of water. With his short hair, white shirt, black tie, and Coke-bottle glasses he looked more like a geek child than a flower child.

Meanwhile, the red-haired girl kept shouting, "What do we want?"

And the crowd kept shouting, "Peace!"

"When do we want it?"

I heard a loud

POP

like someone shooting a gun. This was followed by the

clatter-ing

of a can in front of us that began spraying tons of smoke.

"Gas!" Somebody shouted. "They're teargassing us!

Everyone began screaming and running in all direc-tions. That's when a puff of the gas got into my eyes. They burned like they were on fire and began watering—so bad I could barely see as people all around me shoved and pushed to get out of the way. But they just weren't running from the tear gas. They were running from the police who figured now was a good time to charge into the crowd with their billy clubs.

Don't get me wrong, I'm sure the police were doing the right thing . . . I just wasn't crazy about them doing it to me. People kept screaming and shouting as I kept stumbling, tripping, and eventually falling onto the pavement. I tried getting up, but there were just too many legs and feet running on top of me.

"Help!" I coughed, wiping my eyes, trying to see. I almost made it to my feet but not quite. "Somebody help!"

Unfortunately, all the somebodies were too busy running for their lives. Except one.

A pair of hands pulled me to my feet. Through my watery eyes I made out the white shirt and black tie. It was the geek with the glasses. "Take my hand!" he shouted.

I grabbed his hand and he helped me through the crowd. We raced around students and the police arresting those students. Finally we got to the curb and ducked behind an old VW minivan with a giant peace sign painted on it.

"Are you okay?" he asked.

"Yeah." I coughed and rubbed my eyes.

"No, don't rub. That'll further spread the lachrymator thus irritating the mucous membranes of your eyes even more."

I nodded, blinking through my tears.

"What's your name?" he said.

"Jennifer. Is this . . . April first?"

"All day." He looked past the van to the students fighting in the street.

"And this is the University of Washington?"

He nodded but kept his eyes on the redhead who screamed and put up such a fight that it took two policemen to control her. "Isn't she incredible?" he said.

"Who?"

"Alexis."

I watched as other students were also being arrested, but nobody fought like she did.

"Come on." He took my arm. "We need to get out of here before—"

"All right, hold it right there."

We spun around to see a huge policeman standing behind us. I don't want to say he was big, but if they ever filmed another Incredible Hulk movie he should definitely audition.

"You need to come with me."

My geek friend nodded and pushed up his glasses. "I understand."

Mr. Hulk looked down at me. "You too, missy."

I started to protest, "But I—"

"Come along."

He took both of our arms and moved us toward one of the many waiting police cars.

"Must be a world's record," I sighed.

"For what?" the geek asked.

"For being arrested." I didn't bother to explain that between now, back in Israel, and later in 1961 I'd been arrested three times. It definitely was not one of my better days.

We were in the middle of the street when Alexis, who was struggling not to be shoved into a police car, yelled, "Keep the faith, baby! Keep the faith!"

Mr. Geek shouted back, "You, too, Alexis!"

"Three days!" she yelled as the officers finally pushed her head down and shoved her into the back. "I love you, Bill!"

"I love you too!" Mr. Geek shouted.

As we arrived at our own car, the police officer asked, "Three days for what?"

"Until we are married," the geek said.

"You're marrying *her*?"

"Yes," he sighed, looking over to her car. "Isn't she special?"

The officer snorted, "Well, she's something, I'll give you that."

"Listen, about this girl," Mr. Geek nodded to me. "She's just a child. Can't you let her go?"

The officer gave me a look. I gave him my best puppy dog eyes.

"What's your name?" he asked.

"Jennifer Mackenzie."

He opened the back door and motioned me inside. "Well, Jennifer Mackenzie, until we get things sorted out, you'll have to come with me."

I sighed, nodded and climbed inside. Bill, the geek, followed.

As the officer shut the door, Bill said. "Mackenzie, huh? My last name is Mackenzie."

"That's nice, I said, maybe we're relat—" And then I froze. Slowly, I turned to him. "Bill Mackenzie? You're name is *Bill* Mackenzie?

"That's right."

"As in William Mackenzie? Dr. William Mackenzie?"

He chuckled. "Well, not yet. But someday." He looked back out the window toward Alexis's car.

The name, the kindness, the geekiness—it took nearly a minute to find my voice. "Are you . . . could you . . . what are you studying in college?"

"Archeology?" He caught Alexis's attention and gave her a thumbs-up.

"You're William Mackenzie and you're going to marry *her*?"

"That's right," he beamed. "In two days, nineteen hours and"—he checked his watch—"fifty-one minutes."

"But . . ." I blinked, lost for words. "What . . ." more blinking, ". . . about Mom?"

"Who?"

"Debbie Mackenzie."

He frowned.

"I mean Debbie Simons."

"You know Debbie?"

"Of course I know her, she's my—" I caught myself. "Yeah, we're kinda close."

He smiled. "Sweet kid, isn't she? We've been friends since we were children."

"And you're not going to marry *her*?"

He looked startled. "Why would I marry her?"

"Because you love her."

He scowled as if the thought had never crossed his mind. Our car started up and pulled away. Mr. Geek/Bill/William/Dad caught Alexis's eyes one last time. She blew him a big kiss, smiled, and flashed the peace sign.

"She really is something," Dad sighed.

I closed my eyes trying to clear my head. Like the offi-cer, I had to agree she was definitely something. The only problem was that something was definitely not my mother.

Chapter Twenty-One

THINGS HEAT UP

J
A
K
E

There had to be some way to get Enthal out of here and join her cousin on the ark. Yeah, I know what God said about only saving Noah's family, but maybe Phelmona was right. Maybe Enthal could be the exception. And yeah, I know, I probably had a thing for her. Then, of course, there were a few other obstacles in our way . . . like her being a little older (by three or four thousand years!). And that other minor problem of her being a superplasmatic three-dimensional holographic image. But, other than that, things could work out great for us . . . if she just didn't feel she had to stick around with the rest of her village . . . let alone that big Neanderthal jerk of a boyfriend who

139

had manhandled her last night (and gave me the major migraine).

Speaking of which:

"Woman!" His voice boomed from the back room of their little hut. "What's that noise?"

I could see her getting all tense as she called back, "It's just the storm. I'm sorry."

Sorry? I thought. *For what? The weather?*

"Well, stop it!"

"Yes, of course." Her voice was high and wavy like Jen's gets when she's nervous. "I'll do my best."

I watched as she flitted about the hut, straightening this and that. Then restraightening that and this. Then restraightening the restraightening. Not that it would do much good. I hear worldwide floods can really mess up a place . . . before completely destroying it.

A loud thumping at the doorway brought her to a stop. She turned to see Ham's sister-in-law from next door standing in the opening. The woman's hair was plastered down, soaking wet. She was silhouetted by the fire from the burning tree outside. "We are evacuating to higher ground," she shouted.

Enthal cupped her hands behind her ears to hear over the storm. "What?"

"There is too much water here. We are moving to higher ground where it is safe."

"Woman!" the voice roared from the back room.

Enthal threw a nervous look over her shoulder.

The neighbor shouted, "Tell him we must leave."

"How much time do we have?"

"Now. You must leave *now*."

Enthal thanked her and nodded. The neighbor returned the nod, turned to leave, then turned back. "You cannot stay here, Enthal. With or without him, you must move to higher ground. Now."

"I understand."

They held each other's look another moment before the neighbor turned and disappeared into the night.

"Who was that?" the voice bellowed.

Enthal spun around to see the monster of a man leaning against the bedroom doorway. His hair was mussed, his eyes blurred, and it was all he could do to stand. I've never seen anybody officially hung over (except on TV and stuff), but this guy looked like he had a bad case of it. Or several bad cases.

"Naalamachelruha," she shouted over the storm. (Of course, with a name like that, I'd be cranky too.) "We must move to higher ground."

"I told you, talk to no one without my permission."

"It was only our neighbor."

"You question my authority?"

"No, no, of course not. But she says we must move. On account of the rain we must move to higher ground."

"No one tells me what to do."

"But the rain is coming down so hard." She stepped closer to him. "No one has ever seen such—"

"Never question me!" With one swipe of his meaty arm, the big man hit her, sending her staggering across the room.

Without thinking (one of my specialties) I raced at him and leaped on him. It was just like old times, or at least last night. The good news was this time he didn't crack open my head or rearrange any body parts.

The bad news was he didn't have time because the entire roof of the hut suddenly caved in, crashing down all around us. But it wasn't from the water. Remember that burning tree just outside the hut? Well now it was inside the hut.

Enthal screamed. I screamed. And Naalamachelruha would have too, if one of the ceiling beams hadn't knocked him to the floor in an unconscious heap. I jumped up and raced for the doorway, thanking God that the beam didn't hit me. And while I had His attention, I figured it might be a good time to convince God to, oh, I don't know, MAYBE SAVE MY LIFE!

Smoke was quickly filling the hut—almost as bad as the boy's restroom at school during recess. And where there's smoke, there's fire. Lots of it. Flames shot up the thatched walls until the entire hut was blazing.

"Naalamachelruha!" Enthal was on her hands and knees, coughing, trying to see through the smoke.

There was no answer.

She scrambled to her feet and staggered toward the flames, ducking and dodging pieces of burning roof that were falling. Going farther inside would be suicide. I knew that. But she didn't. Against my better judgment (another one of my specialties) I raced to her, doing my own ducking and dodging until I was able to jump in front of her and shout, "No! You have to get out!" But of course she didn't hear me or see me. (Superplasmatic three-dimensional holographic images can be so stubborn some times.)

Then, deeper inside the hut, through the crackling

fire we heard, every so faintly, "Enthal . . ." Suddenly Mr. Macho sounded more like Mr. Whimpering Cry Baby.

But Enthal fell for it. "I'm coming," she shouted. "Hang on!"

Another chunk of burning roof caved in, knocking her to the ground. Somehow she managed to get to her feet, but only for a second. There was too much smoke and she had to drop back to the floor where she could breathe.

"Enthal . . ."

She crawled on her hands and knees toward the voice, coughing and gagging all the way. "I'm . . . coming." But she ran into a thick wall of fire that blocked her. Their table had tipped over. It was completely engulfed in flames. She tried pushing it aside, but it was just too hot. She turned, looking through the smoke for another way. She saw an opening and started toward it until the rest of the roof caved in, falling all around her. She raised her hand, trying to shield her face from the flames and heat.

"Get out of here!" I shouted. "You have to get out!" I heard crumbling and looked up just in time to see the bedroom wall cave in. I heard the man scream, almost hysterically, then suddenly stop.

Enthal shouted his name.

There was no answer.

She shouted again, coughing and gagging on the smoke. If I didn't do something, she'd go after him. But how could I stop her?

Suddenly, I heard the voice of Ham's brother-in-law from next door. I turned to see he had a wet cloth over his mouth as he staggered through the flames toward us.

"Enthal! You have to go!"

"No," she screamed. "He needs—"

"There's nothing you can do!"

"But he—"

Without a word, the man reached past me and grabbed her around the waist.

"NO!" she cried.

He began pulling her back.

"He needs me, he—" she broke into a fit of coughing as she kicked and fought. But she was no match for him as he threw her over his shoulder and crossed through the flames to the doorway. It seemed like a pretty good idea so I quickly followed.

We barely made it out into the cool air and rain before the last of the walls collapsed, falling into each other, turning the little hut into a giant bonfire.

Chapter Twenty-Two

THIS WILL BLOW YOUR MIND

J
E
N
N
I
F
E
R

"So where are your parents?" Dad asked.

"Um, my mom, she's dead."

"I'm sorry to hear that."

I nodded, knowing he'd be a lot sorrier than he thought.

"And your father?"

Okay, so how does a thirteen-year-old girl tell some nineteen-year-old boy that he's her dad? (If you're looking for a new definition of awkward, I've got it.) But I had to tell him. Like I said to Jesse, he'd definitely be smart enough to figure out how to fix all this. Still, it would require just the right place and just the right time. And somehow, walking out of the city jail after being arrested for four hours, didn't seem like either.

We'd barely stepped outside and onto the steps before we heard the red-headed girl calling, "Hey, Billy boy. Over here, you outrageous piece of grooviness."

We turned to see her waving to us from beside a school bus. It was painted with every colored flower you could imagine—and some you couldn't. A line of students were hugging her and stepping on board, most of them I recognized from the march.

When we arrived, she planted a big romantic kiss on Dad, and when he tried to come up for air, she just kept on kissing. When they broke apart, she laughed, "And that's just the first of my surprises."

Still smiling, she turned to me and said, "Who's the chick?"

"This is Jennifer Mackenzie," he said

"Far out, I'm Alexis." Turning to Dad she said, "You didn't tell me you had a little sister."

"I don't."

"You two sure look related."

If she only knew.

"Did your father post bail to get us out?" Dad asked.

Alexis laughed. "To get *all* of us out." Turning to me, she explained, "My ol' man is like one of the filthiest, richest lawyers in the state. All it took was one little call from his sweet, precious baby girl." She raised her voice, imitating a six-year-old. "Oh Daddy, dearest. Those mean ol' police. They arrested me and all of my beautiful friends . . . and all we were doing was having a little fun." She shook back her hair and laughed, "He's such a pushover."

I'd barely met the girl and already disliked her.

"And the bus?" Dad asked.

She giggled. "He had a little spare change left over. Out of sight, huh?"

Dad nodded.

"Well, get on board and let's begin this magical mystery tour." She reached out and gave my cheek a little pinch. "You, too, Miss Jenny-Jen-Jen."

I was liking her even less.

We climbed into the bus. It was quite a circus. Music blasting, half-naked girls painting the bodies of half-naked boys. More than a few couples were making out and more than that were passing around bottles in brown paper bags and pills that definitely did not look like aspirin.

Dad glanced around, kind of nervous. I glanced around more nervous than kind of. He leaned toward me and said, "Are you going to be okay with this?"

I swallowed. The truth was I wasn't. The bigger truth was neither was he.

"Oh, not back there," Alexis called to us. She motioned to the front seats. "Sit up here with the *looove* queen."

"Right on!" someone yelled. "Sock it to him, sister."

We moved back to the front as the looove queen welcomed every girl that boarded with a hug and every guy with a lingering kiss. I couldn't believe my dad would be involved with something, with someONE like this.

Once we got seated I asked, "You're not serious are you?"

"About what?"

"About marrying *her*." My voice kinda cracked, which I thought was strange.

He smiled shyly. "Actually, that's more Alexis's idea. She asked me."

"She asked *you* to marry *her*?" I cleared my throat. It was like a frog had suddenly moved in.

He nodded.

"And you said yes?" My voice cracked again, getting even lower.

"She's so different from me. So open, so free." He stared at her, getting all dreamy again. "I've never met anyone like her."

"But . . ." My voice dropped even lower. I cleared it and tried again. "She really doesn't seem"—my voice cracked—"your type."

"Are you okay?" he asked. "You're not catching a cold are you?"

I shook my head and cleared my throat again.

"Alrightee!" Alexis shouted to the crowd. "Are all you beautiful people ready to get it on?"

"Cool!" they shouted. "Cosmic! Lay it on me!"

"Out of sight!" Alexis flashed them the peace sign before she plopped down across the aisle from where Dad and I were sitting. She motioned for Dad to join her and started to give me a wink, but stopped. "Jenny-Jen-jen? What happened to your hair?"

"My hair?" My voice croaked.

"Wasn't it brown when you got on board? Far out, that's so cool."

Dad looked at me equally surprised.

"What's wrong?" I pulled my hair in front of my face to look.

"Nothing's wrong," she said. "It's just so—"

"Red?" I cried. "My hair is red!" (And we're not talking average red. It was glow-in-the-dark, neon red.)

Alexis giggled, "Why girl, it's as red as mine. How awesome is that?" She turned to the rest of the bus and shouted. "Look everyone. Look what's happened to her hair."

"Groovy!" someone shouted. "What a trip."

I just kept staring at it, not believing my eyes.

Still laughing, Alexis turned back to me. "Why you and me, Jenny Jen-Jen . . . we could almost be related."

My mind raced. I kept pushing the thought out of my head but it kept pushing its way back in. Was it possible? No! Absolutely not! No way would I become this woman's daughter. If Dad thought he was marrying her, he'd have to think again. I took a deep breath, trying not to panic (which, by now, was a little late). Three days, he'd said. I had three days to get him to change his mind before the wedding. I could do that. I *had* to do that. But how?

I rubbed my head, trying to think. Only then did I notice the size of my hands. I turned them over and to my horror saw thick hair sprouting from my knuckles. Lots of it. Stunned, I looked at my arms. More hair! But there was something else—my arms were getting thicker, more muscular. They no longer looked like some girl's arm, but some guy's!

"Hey, Alexis!" one of the passengers whose entire body was painted in wall-to-wall flowers shouted, "Where we going?"

Alexis flipped her hair to the side and laughed. "To our wedding."

"Wedding?" It was Dad's turn to croak.

Snuggling up to him, she said. "That's my little surprise. Instead of waiting three whole days, we're getting married tonight on the beach."

"Did you hear that?" the painted girl shouted to the others. "They're getting married! Tonight!"

The entire bus cheered. Well, almost the entire bus. It's hard to cheer when you're busy weeping . . . or whatever teenage boys do when they're unhappy.

Chapter Twenty-Three

THE WEDDING

J
E
N
N
I
F
E
R

The sun was just setting over the Seattle beach as I stood with the rest of the wedding party watching Alexis approach the alter (a piece of driftwood with sticks of burning incense stuck into it). Beside us stood the "minister" (some guru guy with a beard down to his belly). For whatever reason Alexis had made me one of her brides-maids—probably because she thought we looked like sisters. Though at the rate I was changing, I might make a better best man.

"Nothing to get uptight about," she'd said earlier as we were getting ready. "Lots of chicks have facial hair. It's just . . ."

"Just what?"

"Well, a full-on beard might be a little over the top."

I tried not to panic (or break into more tears). I still had a few minutes left to fix things. Of course *knowing* how to fix things would make it easier. Somehow, some way, I *had* to convince Dad not to marry Alexis. I glanced over to him. He looked as nervous as a long-tailed cat at a rocking chair convention.

"Are you really sure you love him?" I'd asked her.

She clucked her tongue. "Jenny Jen-Jen."

I glanced down. "Sorry. It just seems—"

"Of course I don't love him."

My head jerked up. "You don't? But then, why . . ."

"Are we getting married?"

I nodded.

"Because he's so uncool he's cute. Not like my other friends. Honestly, have you ever met anyone so square and uptight?"

I bit my lip. After all, she was talking about my father. Sure, he wasn't exactly a party animal and the word *slacker* wasn't even in his vocabulary. But that's what made him so great. That's why he was making all those archeological discoveries. That's why Robbie was helping him with all those inventions.

Alexis continued, "He's just a novelty, Jenny Jen-Jen. A toy."

"You want to be married to a toy?"

She broke out laughing. "Don't freak out. Marriage is just a piece of paper. Trust me"—she gave one of the guy guests who'd been leering at her a wink—"there'll be plenty of boys in my life."

I didn't know whether to slug her or scream or both. "But," I stammered, "he loves you."

"He'll be happy as a clam working in Daddy's law firm. He'll never even know—"

"Law firm? He's going to be a world-famous archeologist."

"Oh, that's what he thinks. But no way am I going to allow that. So no way is he going to be that."

Our little girl talk had been ten minutes ago. And now, as I watched her move through the people to the altar and give Dad a full-flirt smile, I was beside myself, ready to explode. Fortunately, Robbie saved me the trouble. Suddenly he

FLASH

appeared. But instead of the crowd panicking, everybody started murmuring:

"Cosmic."

"Far out"

"Do it again, Daddy-o." (Daddy-o? Okay, he was a *real* old hippie.)

"Robbie!" I rushed to him, "How'd you get here?"

He showed me a time beam generator exactly like mine, then motioned to the dimensional folder he was standing on.

"You made others?"

"Consider it a two for one sale," he said as he reset his time beam generator.

Meanwhile the wedding guests were crowding around for a better look at all the flashing lights.

"Groovy."

"Out of sight."

"You're one cool cat, daddy-o." (Yeah, the same old guy.)

"How's Jake?" I asked.

"The flood has started. We're running out of time."

"Excuse me." Dad stepped up. "Who exactly invited you?"

"Hey Dr. Mackenzie." Robbie snapped the standby switch on the time beam generator and, just like old times, it began to

HUMMM

Pointing it at Dad, he asked, "You ready for a little trip?"

Dad pushed up his glasses. "I beg your pardon."

"Will you step on this platform, please?"

Dad looked down at the platform.

Robbie pointed the generator at him. "Please, boss, don't make me use this."

Dad stared at it, unsure what to do. But the crowd knew:

"Come on, man."

"Don't be a square."

"Expand your mind, man."

Figuring the dimensional folder was probably just a

stupid toy and not wanting to look like a spoiled sport in front of all of Alexis's friends, he finally stepped up onto it.

"Thanks," Robbie said as he hit the button and

CRACKLE

FLASH

Dad was gone.

"Far out!"

"Awesome!"

"Robbie!"

He grinned at me. "Your turn."

"But—"

"It's the only way to straighten out this mess. Let's go. By the way, nice beard."

I stepped onto the platform, he pointed his generator at me and

CRACKLE

FLASH

I was floating at Dad's side, once again traveling through dimensions.

A second later

FLASH

Robbie joined us.

Dad looked pretty nervous and for a good reason. "Will someone please tell me what is happening?"

"Long story," Robbie said. "We gotta fix things here so we can get back and save Jude."

"Jake," I said. "His name is Jake."

"Who's Jake?" Dad asked.

"Your son," I said. "My brother."

Dad's eyes widened. He opened his mouth, then closed it. Then opened it again, but still no words came.

I took his hand. "Sorry, Dad. Like Robbie said, it's a long story."

His mouth twitched as he tried to force it into a hopeful smile. "This is a bad trip, isn't it? Some dream."

"Sorry, Doctor dude," Robbie said. "It's totally real and we haven't much time."

Chapter Twenty-Four

A HELPING HAND

J
E
S
S
E

I woke up in soft mud—which I suppose is better than never waking up on hard rock. Thunder cracked and rumbled nonstop as rain pelted my face. I sat up, wiped my eyes, and peered into the darkness. The zebra that had thrown me was long gone. Now there was only black, except for blinding flashes every few moments as lightning forked and sizzled through the air.

Remembering the chimpanzee, I shouted, "Maximilian?"

There was no answer, just the booming thunder and pounding rain.

"Hey, little guy!"

I spotted something in the big tree just ahead. He sat on the lowest branch silhouetted by the lightning and was shivering and clinging to the tree for all he was worth. My heart went out to him. I knew I had to get Jake, but I also knew I couldn't just leave him there. Yeah, I suppose I'm a softy, but there's not much I can do about it.

I got to my feet and sloshed through the stream of flowing mud, slipping and sliding all the way. It was only two or three inches deep, not like the raging river just on the other side of the tree, but it was still hard to keep my balance.

"It's okay, pal," I shouted. "I'll be right there."

More lightning and thunder. And more shivering.

I finally got to the tree and steadied myself against the trunk so I wouldn't slip and fall into the river. He was about eight feet above me. "It's cool," I shouted. "No worries, come on down."

Maximilian gave me a look that said, "I may be a stupid ape, but I plan to keep on being a living one."

"Come on, fella." Bracing my back against the tree, I reached up toward him. "I've got you."

He cocked his head, thought a moment, then scampered up higher to another branch.

I groaned. "Come on, guy, we gotta get Jake."

He wiped his face, gave one of his famous, "Ooo-ooo, ahh-ahh, eee-eees," and turned away. Not exactly the answer I wanted.

The lowest branch, the one he'd been sitting on earlier, was just above me. Normally, I could jump to it and pull myself up, but with all the slick mud under my feet, I wasn't so sure. Still, I saw no other way. I carefully crouched down and gave a leap. But, just like I feared, my foot slipped and I was falling backward toward the river. I twisted and somehow managed to wrap my arms around the trunk of the tree, dangling just a couple feet above the roaring water.

I kicked and shinnied up the trunk until I leaped to dry land—well, muddy land. It took a moment to catch my balance. When I looked up to Maximilian, he simply stared down at me, unimpressed. I wiped the rain out of my eyes, took a breath, and jumped again. This time I caught the branch and pulled and scrambled until I was sitting on top of it. Maximilian was only a few feet above me now. All I had to do was stand up on the branch and reach up to him. Of course the wet branch was almost as slippery as the mud. But if I used the trunk of the tree for support it would be no problem.

Carefully, I worked my way into a standing position. Then, leaning my back against the tree, I reached for Maximilian. "I'm right here, fella. Come on." He was just inches from me but had no interest in helping. I stepped a little further out, wobbling and teetering, but I was okay. "I'm right here, little guy. I'm right—"

That's when the branch gave a sickening

CRACK

and before I could jump, both it and I fell back into the stream of mud. I slipped and slid, trying to stop myself, but I was moving too fast and the mud was too slick. Within seconds, I shot off the bank and plunged into the river.

I may have yelled, I don't know. It's hard yelling when you've been sucked under water by a powerful current. I wasn't much of a swimmer. Actually, I didn't swim at all—one of the disadvantages of growing up in a desert. I spun and tumbled, trying to get to the surface. But where was it? I managed to bob up once and gulped some air before I was dragged back under. I kept tumbling, having no idea of up or down. Then I saw a faint flash. Lightning. That was all I needed. I fought toward it, kicking and thrashing until, somehow, I made it back to the surface.

I gasped for air just as a giant wave hit my face and suddenly I was breathing water. A lot of it. I panicked. Coughing and choking, I sucked in even more. My lungs were filling with it. *So this is what drowning is like*, I thought. I was pulled back under for what I knew would be the last time. My head grew light, my ears began ringing. Everything was turning white. I was losing consciousness. I no longer felt my arms or legs. I no longer—

Suddenly something grabbed me. A powerful grip began pulling. At first I fought it, but it held me tight until I surfaced, coughing. A moment later my feet hit solid ground. The current was swift and I lost my footing more than once. But I kept climbing until I was finally out of the water, stumbling onto a slick, grassy bank where I collapsed.

Lightning flashed every few seconds. And in it I saw another form beside me, dark and furry. Maximilian was on his hands and knees gagging and gasping for his own breath.

And there as we coughed, sucking in the cool, precious air, I was grateful for two things . . .

1. Maximilian had saved my life.
2. He didn't have to give me mouth to mouth.

Chapter Twenty-Five

DECISIONS, DECISIONS

J
E
N
N
I
F
E
R

As we passed through the lower dimensions (complete with light, feathers, and singing voices), Robbie and I explained to Dad all that had happened. Of course he did a lot of eye blinking and pushed up his glasses a lot, but at least he understood. He may have thought he was still dreaming, or that we were out of our minds, but at least he understood.

"So you sent me back to 1961," he said, "when I was a little boy."

"That's right," I said. "When we were in the elevator. But it was a total accident." My voice was no better. In fact, I sounded deeper than ever. I was afraid to check my face.

"And you're the one who chased me into the street when I got hit by the car."

"You remember that?" I asked.

"Of course I remember it. That was a very strange day." He pushed up his glasses again. "I also remember having an unsettling dream. At least I thought it was a dream—about a boy hiding in the bathroom." He shook his head and continued. "And Debbie; you say I'm supposed to marry Debbie Simons instead of Alexis?"

"It's your choice, dude," Robbie said. I shot him a look and he answered, "We always have a choice. But you might want to check out what you're about to see first."

We'd just risen into the dimension where, a few hours earlier, Jesse couldn't enter without getting burned—the place where the light inside me was as bright as the light outside. I looked over to Dad and Robbie and saw the brightness was also inside of them. *You are pure,* the voices had said, *because you chose the Pure to make you pure.* I breathed a sigh of relief, knowing the two of them must have also made that choice.

The singing around us grew louder and the light rippled until we saw a bunch of those 3D scenes below us. But instead of my life, they were Dad's. Like before, each scene was connected with a beam of green, vibrating light. Sometimes it led to a totally white scene, sometimes to another scene we could see.

"Wow," Dad whispered. "This is some dream."

"No way Dr. Bro," Robbie said. "It's just a higher dimension."

"How's that?"

"Our bodies hang out in three dimensions, but most brainiac physicists figure we're surrounded by at least twenty-two."

"Twenty-two dimensions?" Dad could only shake his head in wonder before looking back down. "And those white sections?"

"Lame stuff you did that you want forgotten."

I turned to Robbie. "You've been here before?"

He motioned to the dimensional folder. "I invented this thing, remember?"

He had a point.

Spotting a specific scene, he said, "Check it out, Dr. Dude, there's your wedding."

We looked down and, sure enough, there was the wedding we'd just come from. And after a few of those connecting beams, there was another scene of Dad working away in a tiny cubicle.

"What's that?" Dad asked.

"I'm just guessing," I said, "but Alexis told me you'd be working in her father's law office."

Dad scoffed, "I'm going to be an archeologist."

"The scenes don't lie," Robbie said.

"But my whole life, that's all I've ever dreamed of."

"Sorry, Doc."

And we were sorry. All of us.

Dad spotted another scene and pointed. "And that?"

Now, I don't want to be judgmental or anything, but Alexis was in this scene and she looked awful. She was skeleton-skinny, her hair was a mess, and it looked like she hadn't changed clothes in weeks. She and Dad were arguing, really going at it. By the stack of bills he dropped on the table, I'm guessing it was about money. And with the syringe I caught a glimpse of in Alexis's hand and the drugs scattered all around the filthy table, you didn't have to be a genius to understand why. She had become an addict, and it looked like all their money was going to her habit.

I could hear Dad groaning beside me. "I can't believe it. This is terrible."

No argument there.

"And that." He pointed to another scene. "Look at that."

It was even worse. The same dirty and messy Alexis was robbing some convenience store with a gun in her hand.

We stared in disbelief.

After that scene there were several white ones where we saw nothing at all. And next to them was another. Grandma Mackenzie was on a porch holding the hand of a little boy with red hair sobbing and crying his eyes out.

"I think that's . . ." Robbie leaned forward for a closer look. "Jen, I think that's you."

Oh brother, I thought. *How can this get any worse?*

I was about to find out.

The scene shifted slightly and we saw the reason I was crying so hard. Both Dad and Alexis were being led away in handcuffs to a police car.

"That's enough," Dad said. "I don't want to see any more."

"Sorry about that," Robbie said.

"But it doesn't have to be that way?" It was more of a question than a statement.

Robbie answered, "We've always got choices."

Dad turned to me. "And Debbie. Things would be better with Debbie?"

I nodded. "About a thousand times." I didn't have the heart to tell him of Mom's death. But even at that, he'd be mega-times happier. As we watched, the song around us started to change its tune.

"Okay folks," Robbie said. "We're coming up to the darker dimensions."

"Darker dimensions?" Dad asked.

"This is the part where we close our eyes," I said.

"Why? What is it?"

"Trust me. It's a lot easier this way."

"But—"

"We don't have the faith, yet."

He looked at me.

"Better trust her, Doc. It gets real ugly if you don't."

I gave him a nod of encouragement. After glancing back to Robbie, who'd already closed his eyes, Dad finally did the same. So did I. And just in time. Almost immediately the light around us grew redder and darker.

"Is that growling?" Dad asked. "Do I hear growling?"

"Keep your eyes closed," I said. "We're just about there." Even as I spoke, the growling and red flickering started to fade. A moment later it was replaced by the quiet and soothing sound of—

"A hospital?" Robbie said. "We're in a hospital?"

I opened my eyes. We were in the same room I'd left Dad in just a few hours earlier. And there, over in the bed, he slept—well, the eight-year-old, "Billy" version of him slept. I glanced over to the grown up version who was already moving toward him, slow and cautious.

"This is . . . me?" he whispered.

"Looks like," Robbie said.

Little Billy stirred, then opened his eyes. We all froze like we hoped we were wearing invisibility cloaks or something.

His little voice croaked, "Who are you?"

"I'm, uh," Dad glanced to us for help, then answered. "I'm . . . you."

But instead of freaking, Billy just blinked and said, "Oh." He turned to Robbie, then to me. Remembering his last little run in with me, he tensed.

"Don't worry," Dad said, "it's all right. She's, uh, she's, um . . ."

"I'm your daughter."

He looked to me, then to Dad, then back to me. "Oh, okay."

I turned to Dad. "'Oh, okay'?"

Dad shrugged. "For all these years, I just thought it was a dream."

"You remember this?"

"Of course."

Meanwhile, Robbie had pulled out his time beam generator and was adjusting the dial ever so slightly. "Listen, Dr., er, Billy. I'm going to point our cool little flashlight at you, okay?"

"Hold it," I said. "If you send him back home, there won't be a Billy here and Dad will never have been a kid or gone to school or—"

"No problemo, kiddo. I'm just moving him two seconds into the future. When I fire mine, you point and fire yours, and there'll be two of him just a couple seconds apart."

"But there already are two of us," Billy said.

We looked at him

"What do you mean, little dude?"

He leaned past us and called over to the bathroom, "You still in there?"

We turned to look.

"Hey, you still there?"

Ever so slowly the door opened and there before us stood another Billy. "Wow," the new Billy said, "I thought you guys would never come."

We all traded glances.

"You know us?" Robbie asked.

"Of course I know you, you sent me back here." He stepped out of the bathroom and approached. "Did you repair the time beam generator?"

"Good as new, Boss," Robbie said.

"Dad?" I asked.

"What?" all three of them answered.

I rubbed the stubble on my face. This was getting confusing.

"Don't worry," Billy number one said, "it's all just a dream. It'll be over soon."

"Let's hope so," Geek Dad agreed.

"You can say that again," Billy number two said.

"Do we have to?" Billy number one asked.

This wasn't helping my confusion.

Robbie was already repositioning his cross-dimensional folder on the floor. "Okay, Dr. Mackenzie." He looked to Geek Dad. "We need you to step back on this platform again."

"You're sending me back to 1971?"

"For sure, bro."

"By myself?" He sounded a little worried.

"No biggie," Robbie said as the lights began flashing. "Just keep your eyes shut and you'll be there, no sweat."

He hesitated just a second before finally stepping onto the platform.

"Dad." Before I could stop myself I ran to him and give him a hug. He returned it, more than a little awkward. Then holding me out at arm's length, he smiled. "I'm going to have a terrific daughter, aren't I?"

Tears filled my eyes as I looked up to him.

He also looked kind of misty-eyed. "See you in a few decades?"

I nodded.

"Hate to break up the party," Robbie said, "But we've got a lot to do."

"Like saving my son," Geek Dad said.

"Like saving your son."

"Wait a minute, what's that mean?" Billy number two asked.

"First things first," Robbie said.

I stepped back as the lights on the cross-dimensional folder flashed faster. "Tell Mom hi for me," I said.

"If she'll have me."

I grinned. "Oh, she'll have you."

Robbie pointed the time beam generator at him. "See you around, Doc."

Dad lifted his hand to wave and

CRACKLE

FLASH

he was gone.

"You think he'll do the right thing?" I asked. "With Alexis I mean?" I was surprised to hear how my voice suddenly sounded a lot higher.

Robbie chuckled. "Yes, he will."

"How can you be so sure?"

"Check out your face."

I reached up and touched my bare skin. My wonderful, smooth, lovely, bare skin. I looked to my arms and hands, which were also thinning down.

"One down, two to go," Robbie said. He turned to Billy number two. "I'm sending you to the staging area."

"What? Why?"

"Jake's lost in there," I said. "We can't find him."

"Jake?"

Robbie nodded. "The flood is already happening. The more manpower we have to find him, the better." He pointed the time beam generator at him. "You ready?"

Billy number two nodded. "Oh, wait." He felt his pockets and pulled out the keys to the pickup we'd left back at the police station. "We will probably need these at some point."

"Smile purty." Robbie pulled the trigger and

FLASH

we were down to one Billy.

Robbie wasted little time in resetting the generator. "Okay, little dude, we gotta run." He motioned for me to step on my dimensional folder as he stepped onto his own. Turning the generator around to face us he said, "Be cool, Doc. We'll catch you in about fifty years."

"Sweet dreams," I said. The little boy nodded, closed his cute, little eyes and

CRACKLE

FLASH

Chapter Twenty-Six

HANGING ON

J
E
S
S
E

We'd barely caught our breath, before Maximilian sat up and started doing his Ooo-oo, ahh-ahh, eee-eee thing.

"What's goin' on, fella?"

He scampered to his feet and looked up the river.

"Right. That's where we were. But now we have to find Jenny's brother."

"Ooo-ooo-ahh-ahh-eee-eee."

"Sorry, pal, my Chimpanzee is a little rusty."

"Ooo-ooo, ahh-ahh, eee-eee." His English wasn't much better. But the way he kept chattering and staring up river, I knew something was going on. I stood up and joined him. Then I heard it too. Voices. Over the thunder, wind, and rain there were voices screaming and yelling. And one sounded very familiar.

"Jenny!"

They grew louder. I squinted up the river until I saw them—a group of people, bobbing up and down. If someone didn't get out there and help pull them in, they'd drown. And since there weren't a whole lot of volunteers, I guessed that someone was me. I wasn't excited about getting back into the river, but like I said, there was no one else. I took a step into the water, but Maximilian immediately grabbed my leg with those long, ape arms of his.

"What are you doing?" I tried to shake him off. "Let go!" But he didn't let go. In fact he held on all the tighter. I knew he was trying to protect me, but he obviously didn't know that was Jenny out there.

I kept trying to move but he hung on, his extra 120 pounds definitely not helping. "Maximilian!" I reached down to pry him off but his grip was like steel. I'd heard chimpanzees were supposed to be strong but this was ridiculous. Then, to further make his point, he bent down and bit my hand.

"Ow! What are you doing?"

"Ooo-ooo, ahh-ahh, eee-eee."

I turned back to the river. The group was closer, about forty yards away. I started waving my arms. "Here!" I shouted. "Over here!"

If they heard, they didn't let on.

I turned to Maximilian. "Will you let go, you stupid ape!"

If *he* heard he didn't let on. Instead, he motioned to a

giant branch sticking out into the rushing water. "Ooo-ooo, ahh-ahh, eee-eee! Ooo-ooo, ahh-ahh, eee-eee!"

I didn't understand, until he started dragging me toward it. Then I got the message. Of course, it made perfect sense. I'd hang onto the branch and work my way out into the river to catch them. (Okay, maybe he wasn't the stupid one.)

I waded against the powerful current until I reached the branch and grabbed hold. I looked back up the river and could now see there were three of them—two men and a girl. And they were closer. *A lot* closer. Hanging onto the limb, I made my way further out into the river. Using his chimpanzee balance, Maximilian climbed on top of the branch and walked behind me.

"Guys!" I shouted. Jen! Over here!" I kept going deeper and deeper until my feet no longer touched bottom. "Jen!"

"There!" One of the men yelled. "Someone's over there!" They began splashing toward me.

"It's Jesse!" I shouted as I reached the end of the branch. "Swim over here! I'll catch you!"

I saw their faces plainly now. They were struggling to keep their heads above water. Robbie was in the lead, followed by Jenny's dad, then Jenny—everyone madly splashing in my direction.

"Ooo-ooo, ahh-ahh, eee-eee!"

"Right," I said. I wrapped my left arm around the branch and reached out as far as I could with my right. They were nearly there. Just a few yards away. It was going to be close.

"Hang on!" Robbie said. "Here I come."

"I got you," I shouted, bracing myself for impact.

When he hit, he hit hard, knocking the wind out of me. But even as we made contact, he was turning around to grab Jenny's dad who immediately slammed into him.

Now there was only Jenny.

She was further out and her dad had to stretch for all he was worth—one hand hanging on to Robbie, the other reaching for his daughter. But even where I was, I could see she wasn't going to make it.

"More, Jen!" he shouted. "Come closer!"

She kicked and splashed until, at the very last second, he managed to grab her arm. Actually, the sleeve of her arm.

"Don't let go!" she screamed. "Daddy don't—"

"Take my arm!" he yelled.

But she was too far away to get a good hold.

"Daddy, don't let go!"

"I won't!" You could hear the strain in his voice. "I won't!"

"Hang on to her!" Robbie shouted.

But no amount of shouting helped. His grip was definitely loosening.

"Daddy!"

Suddenly, I felt Maximilian climbing over my shoulders, then jumping onto Robbie's.

"What's he doing!" Robbie shouted. "Get off me, you stupid ape!"

But, once again Maximilian was proving he was anything but stupid. From Robbie's shoulders he leaped onto Jenny's dad.

"Maximilian, get off!"

The chimp paid no attention as he crossed over to Dr. Mackenzie's far shoulder. Then, wrapping one of those long arms around the man's head, he reached out the other to Jenny.

"Take his hand!" I shouted. "Take it!

Jenny let out a cry as she lunged for him. They barely connected . . . then began slipping apart.

"Hang on!" her dad shouted.

Maximilian grunted under the strain but he did not let go. Jen kicked and squirmed until she was able to grab him with her free hand. She pulled herself up his arm toward us. I could hear him breathing and snorting against the pain, but he would not let go. When she was close enough, he wrapped his arm around her and pulled her in for her dad to take hold. And, with Robbie's help, they all moved in and joined me at the branch.

There was plenty of gasping and coughing, but we were all too tired to talk. We followed the branch to the shore where we collapsed onto the grass. Everyone finally safe.

Everyone but Jake.

Chapter Twenty-Seven

SHAKE, RATTLE, AND ROLL

J
E
N
N
I
F
E
R

It was great to see Jesse again. It was also pretty cool not to have drowned. Actually, I'm a good swimmer. It was just all that choking and breathing water that I wasn't so fond of. Unfortunately, the river wasn't quite done with us. Because, even as we lay there, catching our breath, it was rising. In less than a minute, it began lapping around us.

"We better get to higher ground," Dad shouted over the wind and rain. He motioned to the hill behind us. And even though we were bone-weary and more than a little damp, we got to our feet and sloshed toward it.

"What about Jake?" I asked.

"The dude can't be far," Robbie said. "My best guess is he's moved to the top of this hill."

"Pretty convenient," Jesse said.

"Not really. Remember the staging area is small. The rest of this is just illusion."

"Pretty convincing illusion," Jesse said as he flipped his dripping hair out of those incredible blue eyes.

"Thanks, I am an awesome inventor, aren't I."

I tried but it was impossible not to roll my eyes.

We started the steep climb. Robbie took the lead followed by Dad and Maximilian. Jesse and I brought up the rear. Even though the way was covered in bushes and undergrowth, it was pretty slippery because of all the little streams flowing down and around us. Then there were the earthquakes. As a Californian they didn't bother me much—except they kept coming faster and stronger.

"So, Dr. Mackenzie," Jesse shouted. "This whole Noah and the Bible thing, it really happened?"

Dad nodded. "It's not just in the Bible. Ancient writings from other civilizations also speak of a cataclysmic flood covering the earth."

Another earthquake hit, so powerful that I slipped and grabbed Jesse's hand for support. It wasn't the most romantic moment in human history, but it was something we both noticed . . . then pretended we didn't.

When it finally stopped, Jesse shouted up to Dad, "But how? No disrespect, but how can a rainstorm, no matter how big, flood the whole earth?"

"It wasn't just rain," Dad yelled back. "According to Genesis, 'all the springs of the great deep burst forth.'"

"What, like geysers and stuff?"

"Springs, underground rivers, you name it."

The hill we were climbing was finally leveling off when I noticed something off in the distance. "What's that?"

"Where?" Jesse said.

"To the right. It looks like fire. Torches or something."

Everyone turned to see. It was hard to make out through the rain, but as we got closer we saw it wasn't just torches, it looked like—

"People?" Dad asked. "Are those people?" Without waiting for an answer, he raced the last few yards up the hill. "Jake? Jake, are you there?"

Another earthquake struck, harder than the others. The ground heaved so violently that it threw everyone down. With it came a deafening

CRAAAAAAACK!

It sounded like wood splitting or cloth ripping, but a billion times louder. Trees began falling. The earth shifted then became like liquid. Dirt, bushes, boulders, everything began sliding past me. A giant crack appeared out of nowhere and separated me from the group. As it spread, everything on my side began pouring down into it.

Everything including me!

I screamed, trying to scramble up. But the earth tilted higher as the ground kept crumbling and sliding away. It was a losing battle. Like climbing up water. The faster I scrambled, the more the earth under me disappeared. I was being swallowed alive!

Over my scream I heard another roar. Different. Like a giant waterfall. I threw a look over my shoulder and saw a river exploding from the crack. It spewed and sprayed, rising to my ankles, then my waist, then my chest. I was no longer falling but being thrown up and forward. There was only water now. No ground. Just water pushing and shoving. It's like I'd caught the world's biggest wave, a surfer but without a board.

I fought to keep my head above the water as broken trees, dirt, and rocks churned all around. A giant branch tumbled toward me. I screamed, barely ducking in time. A bush slapped my face, gouging into my cheek, blocking my vision. I ripped it away just in time to see a cliff with a gigantic boulder jutting from it. I turned and dove under water, but I was too slow. The rock came straight at me. I raised my arms to cover my head . . .

And then there was nothing at all.

Chapter Twenty-Eight

HOPELESS

J
A
K
E

Even before the giant earthquake, things weren't looking so great.

For starters, we were all huddled together on that stupid hilltop. Well, the few of us who hadn't been washed away when the flood hit the village . . . Phelmona's brother and sister-in-law, four or five others, and of course, Enthal who was still broken up about losing her man. Even though there were only a few of us left, it didn't stop the fights and arguments. I'm guessing losing friends and loved ones can make you kinda cranky. And realizing you're next on the list probably doesn't help.

So as the water rose higher and higher, the tempers got hotter and hotter:

"Why would Noah's god do this to us?" one old guy demanded.

"Why did we choose to do it to ourselves?" Phelmona's brother countered.

"You're as crazy as he is. None of us chose to die!"

"Of course we did. When we chose to ignore his warnings." The brother looked down the hill to the rising river where his home had been just a few hours earlier. "I chose to keep my possessions . . . and now I've lost everything."

"His god should have made us obey!"

"Why? So we could accuse him of controlling us? No, we got exactly what we wanted."

The veins in the old guy's neck bulged, and it looked like he was going into attack mode (which would have been a suicide mission). But it didn't matter, we'd all be dead in a few minutes anyway. I wondered if a superholographic death would be as real as a superholographic flood. Either way, dead was dead. And like the others, I had no one to blame but myself.

I looked over to Enthal. It wasn't her fault I was here. I'm the one who thought I could help by hanging back. Stupid? You bet. Helpful? Guess again. But it was weird, even now, with all that was going on, I still hurt for her. Unlike Phelmona's brother, she wasn't dying because she wanted to hold on to stuff. She was dying because she wanted to fit into the crowd. The only problem was everyone in the crowd was dead or soon would be.

I took a breath for courage. It didn't help. And then I heard over the storm: "Jake?" Someone was calling. "Jake, are you there?"

I spun around and, was it my imagination, or was that Dad sloshing his way up the hill to me? I started to shout back when we were suddenly hit with another earthquake. The big one. So powerful, everybody was thrown to the ground. It heaved and lunged until the whole side of the hill opened up like someone unzipping a giant crack in the ground. It didn't stop, but just kept getting wider and longer. By the time I got to my hands and knees it was racing up the hill toward me, sucking down all the rocks and trees. It was like watching one of those Norway fjords being formed . . . heading straight for yours truly!

I rolled out of the way, and just in time. The crack raced past me only a couple yards away and kept going across the hill. As it widened I leaped to my feet and ran for all I was worth. I could hear all sorts of smashing and falling and crashing behind me.

Then the water came. It shot up like a geyser. But because it gushed out from the side of the hill and not the top where I was, I was safe.

Over the roar, I heard the faint sound of screaming. I looked down to my right and just twenty feet below was my sister! The water had picked her up and was sending her flying through the air.

"Jenny!"

She was twisting and tumbling like a cork, sometimes under the water, sometimes on top, always fighting to catch her breath. I spotted the giant boulder a split second before she did.

"Jenny, look—"

She slammed head first into it and disappeared under the water.

"JENNY!" I was frantic, searching for any trace of her when—there, off to the side—I spotted her. She'd been flung to the shallow edge of the water. I scrambled toward her. The water had receded but only for a minute. It was quickly filling the valley below and was rising again. I half slid, half fell as dirt and rocks clattered down with me until I was at her side.

She lay face down, not moving. I pulled her out and flipped her over. Her eyes stared lifelessly, her face was covered in blood.

"No!" I shook her. "Jenny!"

Fighting the panic, I laid the back of her head in the mud and tilted up her mouth.

"Hang on, Jen!"

I scooped the mud out of her mouth, my hands shaking. "Don't go, don't go!"

Just like I'd seen in the movies, I pinched her nose and took a breath. I put my mouth over hers and blew.

Nothing.

I took another breath and tried again. Then again. "You can't leave me!"

Hot tears on my face mixed with the cold rain. "I won't let you!" I tried again, then again. But she would not wake up.

"Jenny, no! Jenny, come back! JENNY . . ."

Chapter Twenty-Nine

REWIND, RESET, REDO . . . REAL FAST!

J
E
S
S
E

By the time we'd crossed around the giant crack in the ground and reached Jen's side, things were bad, real bad. Dr. Mackenzie had already dropped to his knees at her side and was shouting to Jake. "How long has she been unconscious?"

But Jake was crying too hard to answer.

Robbie kneeled at her other side trying to find her pulse.

"Jake, how long has she been unconscious?"

More tears. "I . . . she's . . ."

"I don't have a pulse, Doc," Robbie yelled. "She's not breathing."

The doctor looked to him in alarm then immediately bent over and started giving her mouth to mouth.

"It won't do any good," Jake sobbed. "I've tried. Dad, she's . . . she's . . ." He couldn't say the word.

"Not yet," Robbie said, rising to his feet. "Technically, she's not dead until her brain is, and that takes a good six, maybe seven minutes with no oxygen."

"So she's alive?" Jake asked.

"As long as her brain is. She stopped breathing at least two minutes ago. That gives us five minutes, tops." He reached to his wristwatch and set the timer.

"Five minutes to do what?" Dr. Mackenzie asked.

"To straighten out this mess." Robbie pulled the small platform for the dimensional folder from his coat and unfolded it.

"I hope that's waterproof," I said.

"Of course, I thought of everything."

It looked pretty beat up but when he turned it on all the lights began to flash. His time beam generator wasn't so lucky. He barely had it out of his other pocket before he groaned.

"What's wrong?" I asked.

"It's jammed. Hand me Jenny's."

I hesitated.

"Hurry! We haven't much time."

I reached down and pulled the generator from her coat pocket. When I passed it to him, he looked at the dials and sighed. "It's almost out of power. Jake?"

But Jake was still crying.

"Jake, listen to me!"

He finally looked to him.

"I don't have enough power to send you all the way back to before you fell off that pole into the staging area. But if we're lucky I can transport you to earlier this morning. Will that give you enough time to find the ark?"

Jake thought a second then wiped his face and nodded. "I can follow Ham and his wife back, but how will that help?"

"We'll send Jesse to come get you."

"We'll do what?" I asked.

"I'll explain later." He turned to Jake. "You ready?"

Jake nodded and got to his feet.

"You'll see yourself there, but stay out of sight or you'll mess things up. That first reality you lived has to play itself out."

Dr. Mackenzie looked up from his daughter, his voice hoarse with emotion. "I sure hope you know what you're doing?"

Robbie muttered, "Me, too, boss. Me too." As he spoke he turned on the generator. It began **HUMMM**-ing and the multicolored lenses spun.

"If we want to save Jenny, every second counts, so . . ." He pulled the trigger and

FLASH

Chapter Thirty

TICK . . . TICK . . . TICK . . .

J
A
K
E

00:04:10

Suddenly, I was back outside Enthal's hut watching my old self watch her as she handed Phelmona, Ham's wife, those two shivering puppies. I stepped further into the darkness so my old self couldn't see me. (No need giving myself a heart attack.)

Just like before, Enthal croaked out an emotional, "Good-bye, cousin."

And, just like before, Phelmona looked at her one last time before nodding then turning with Ham to head back to the ark.

Of course my old self shouted at her, trying to convince her to go, but of course she couldn't hear. I wanted to run up and join in the yell fest, but it would be pointless. No matter what we said or did, nothing would change her mind. We watched helplessly as she turned and headed back to the hut.

My old self followed her.

But I turned and started after Ham and Phelmona. God had known all along. Only Noah and his family would be saved.

Chapter Thirty-One

COUNTING DOWN

J
E
S
S
E

00:03:47

I turned to Robbie. "Now what?"

"We have three minutes and forty-seven seconds left. Now we go to the hospital."

"The what? That's crazy."

"Jenny's generator is out of juice and mine is jammed. It can only go back one setting at a time."

I turned to Dr. Mackenzie who was already thinking it through and nodding.

"You first," Robbie said. "We'll just use the time beam generator so you don't have to cross dimensions."

"Right."

"But you'll be a kid again."

"No problem."

"We'll follow you with our generator and dimensional folder."

"What about Jen?" I asked.

"She'll come with us. Can you carry her?"

I nodded.

He turned back to her dad. "You set?"

Dr. Mackenzie nodded.

"We'll see you in a minute." Robbie pointed the time beam generator at him and

FLASH

he was gone.

Now he turned to me. "Okay, carry Jennifer to the platform." He motioned to Maximilian. "Ape man and I will follow."

I picked up Jenny and carried her in my arms to the dimensional folder. Once I stepped onto it, Robbie hit the switch and

CRACKLE

FLASH

00:03:02

After quickly traveling through dimensions, the four of us arrived back in the hospital—Robbie, Jenny, Maximilian, and me. But instead of one eight-year-old Dr. Mackenzie, there were two of them—one boy in the bed, the other standing beside him.

"What's going on?" I asked.

"Don't worry," the boy in bed said. "It's just another weird dream."

Robbie turned to the other boy. "You were just with us in the staging area?"

"That is correct."

Robbie aimed the generator at him. "See you soon."

"Here we go again," the little guy sighed as

FLASH

he disappeared.

Robbie then turned the generator onto Jenny and me. "You still standing on the dimensional folder?" he asked.

I nodded.

"Bye-bye."

CRACKLE

FLASH

00:02:18

Once again we traveled dimensions. I held Jenny in my arms the whole way. But when we landed we weren't back home in the lab tent, we were on a beach at sunset. It made no sense. Obviously, Robbie had made a mistake because all around us were these long-haired, hippie types. And directly beside me stood not one, but two younger and thinner Dr. Mackenzies. And while we're not making sense, there was also another Jenny. Only this Jenny had red hair. She was in the back so busy talking to another red-headed woman that she didn't see us pop in, which was probably just as well.

"Who are you?" the first Dr. Mackenzie was asking the second.

"I'm you?" the other said.

Spotting me, the first Dr. Mackenzie asked, "And who are you?"

Before I could answer, Robbie and Maximilian also popped into the picture.

"Groovy," a nearby hippie whispered.

"I think I'm trippin,'" another added."

Looking at both Dr. Mackenzies, Robbie asked, "Doc, where are you?"

"Right here, Robbie." The second Mackenzie raised his hand.

"Cool." Robbie turned to the first Mackenzie and grinned. "Remember me when you start hiring in a few dozen years." He pointed the time beam generator at the second and

FLASH

"Awesome," another hippie whispered. "Blow my mind."

Then he pointed it at Jenny and me and

CRACKLE

FLASH

00:01:45

Moments later Robbie and Maximilian joined us all in the lab tent.

"How much time?" Dr. Mackenzie asked.

Robbie glanced at his watch. "One minute, forty-one seconds."

I looked down to Jenny still in my arms. "Why isn't she breathing? We're home."

"You are, she's not." He turned to her dad. "Doc?"

The man was nodding. "We've got to go all the way back to the elevator, don't we?"

"It's the only way to untangle the knot."

"So what can I do?" I asked. Maximilian reached up and took my hand. "What can *we* do?"

Dr. Mackenzie answered. "Jake should be on that ark by now. We still have to remove him from it."

Robbie turned to me. "Go to the control console at the Machine. Ask to borrow Gita's smart phone."

"What good will a smart phone—"

"It has GPS. Take it to the pole Jake fell off of, memorize the coordinates, then jump into the staging area."

"You want me to go back into the program!"

"With the GPS you can lead him out."

Dr. Mackenzie added, "We'll return shortly."

"And Jenny?" I asked.

"By going to the beginning and unwinding all the mess, hopefully we can change her future."

"*Hopefully?*"

"Oh, and Jesse, you're twelve seconds behind yourself."

"What's that mean?"

"It means you've got to run to catch up and tackle the first Jesse that was here earlier."

"Tackle the first—"

"And do it hard. If you hit yourself hard enough, you'll cross the time barrier and become one . . . hopefully."

It sounded crazy, but what else was new. Besides, I remembered what happened when Jen and I collided into our identical selves earlier when we'd folded through dimensions.

"Let's go!" Robbie said. "We've got one minute and sixteen seconds!"

I handed Jenny's limp body over to him. Her skin was turning a creepy blue from lack of oxygen.

"One minute, twelve seconds," he shouted. "Go!"

I ran out of the tent as fast as I could, Maximilian at my side. And there, just a few dozen yards ahead of me was . . . me. I thought of shouting, telling me to wait up. But since I don't remember seeing me the first time, I figured I shouldn't . . . or didn't, or . . . never mind. The point is, I dug in and sprinted forward for all I was worth.

Then, just before we rounded the tents and entered the staging area, I leaped at me. We hit hard and tumbled to the ground. And when we scrambled to our feet, well, there was no longer a we . . . just me.

00:00:52

Like before, the staging area was filled with the raging storm. I ran to the nearby control panel shouting, "Gita! Gita, can I borrow your phone?"

Gita, Hazel, and the Robbie from before looked up

from their work. So did the other Maximilian. The chimp stopped chewing his little gobs of electrical tape and stared at my other Maximilian who just stared back.

"Oh no," I quietly groaned.

"Oh lookie," Hazel clapped her hands. "You brought Maxi a playmate!"

The two animals kept staring at each other.

"Hey dude," Robbie said, "where's your woman?" It was the exact question he'd asked me before.

"My what?"

"Your babe, your chick, your numero uno momma. You two weren't fooling around with my time beam generator were you?"

I pretended not to hear. Turning to Gita, I asked, "Can I check out your phone? It'll only be a minute."

Robbie took my silence as a yes. "Not cool, dude." He rose from the console. "Didn't I tell you to hold off and I'd get Dr. Mackenzie? Time travel is definitely not for newbies." He was not happy as he headed for the lab tent.

"Isn't he fantastic?" Hazel sighed, gazing after him. "There's nothing he can't do."

Everything was exactly the same, including Maximilian's loud

BUUUURP . . .

Meanwhile, Gita had reached into her pocket and pulled out her phone. "Why do you wish to use it?"

"It has GPS, right?"

"Certainly." She handed it to me. "What are your intention—"

Before she could finish, I spun around and ran toward the staging area. Maximilian stayed at my side. Spotting him, the other Maximilian also took off, no doubt wanting to play a nice game of ape tag.

"Sweetie," Hazel cried after him, "come back!"

"Jesse?" Gita called.

I arrived at the staging area but saw a hundred poles. "Maximilian," I shouted. "Which one did Jake fall off of?"

He veered to the right and I followed.

"Jesse, stop!" Gita shouted. "It is too dangerous!"

Then I spotted one that was bent and broken. "Is that it? Maximilian, is that—"

"Ooo-ooo, ahh-ahh, eee-eee!"

We ran to it and I began climbing. Maximilian followed. "No, boy," I shouted over the storm. "You stay here."

He refused to listen until the other Maximilian arrived and leaped up to grab his foot. "Ooo-ooo, ahh-ahh, eee-eee!"

My Maximilian replied, "Ooo-ooo, ahh-ahh, eee-eee!"

They fell hard to the ground just as I reached the top of the pole. Then, after double-checking the GPS location, I paused a second to gather my courage and jumped into the howling storm.

Chapter Thirty-Two

TIME'S UP

J
A
K
E

00:00:31

It was great to be back on the ark, even with all the fleas

chomp, chomp, chomp-ing

and me

scratch, scratch, scratch-ing.

The water had gotten pretty high and it looked like we'd start floating any second. I raced past Ham and Phelmona and made a beeline downstairs for the stall I'd first landed in. It was a bit crowded thanks to the new tenants—not one, but two African elephants. And don't even get me started on the smells. I'm sure Ham, Phelmona, and the rest of the fam were glad to be safe. But as I sidestepped the mounds of manure, I knew it wasn't exactly going to be a pleasure cruise for them.

I'd barely arrived before

FLASH

Jesse popped in.

"Glad you could make it." I said. Suddenly the boat shuddered and lurched forward. "We've launched. How much time do we have?"

Jesse checked the cell phone in his hand. "Twenty seconds."

"How are we—"

"This thing's got a GPS for getting us out of here. Come on!"

We raced out of the stall and up the ladders to the top deck, all the time Jesse reading the coordinates. We followed them to the far side of the ark.

"Oh no," he groaned. "This can't be right."

"What's wrong?"

He pointed to the water below us. "It says that's our exit coordinates."

"In the water?"

He nodded.

"Then let's go!" I went to the edge, ready to jump in. But when I turned to him, he wasn't moving. "What's wrong?"

"I can't swim," he said.

"Doesn't matter. If that's the exit point, we'll land outside the staging area onto the ground!"

Jesse looked down at the water, anything but thrilled.

"Come on!" I shouted. "We don't have time. Jump!"

He was still frozen.

"For Jenny," I shouted. "We've got to jump for Jenny and we gotta jump now!"

He took a deep breath. "Okay," he said as he stepped up beside me. "But if we die, you're going to live to regret it."

I counted, "One . . . two . . . three . . ."

−00:00:41

The good news was we didn't land in water.

The bad news was hard sand is a lot more painful than soft water.

We scrambled to our feet but Jenny and Dad weren't around. "Where are they?" I yelled.

Gita, Hazel, and not one, but two chimpanzees looked at me, having no idea what I meant.

"I said where—"

FLASH

−00:00:47

Suddenly Dad appeared, holding Jenny in his arms. He dropped to his knees and carefully laid her on the ground.

"How much time?" I asked.

He ignored me and started pumping her chest.

"How much time?"

Jesse glanced at the timer on his cell and muttered. "We're way over."

"How much?"

"Almost a minute."

If Dad heard, he didn't let on. "Come on, sweetheart." He kept pumping. "Come on."

The rest of the team gathered around. I could feel my throat getting tight and my eyes filling with tears. "Please," I choked, "don't let her die." I guess it was a prayer, cause Gita and Hazel were doing the same thing:

"Please, God . . . Please, Lord."

Dad stopped to wipe the sweat off his face or the tears from his eyes. Or both.

"Don't stop!" Jesse shouted. "Don't give up."

Dad nodded and went back to work.

I don't know how much time passed. It could have been five seconds, it could have been five minutes . . . but Jenny's body suddenly convulsed. It did it again. Dad turned her head just as she hurled a bunch of water. Lots of it. She started choking and coughing. More hurling. Finally she gasped in a wheezing, ragged breath. And then another.

We all started to clap or cheer. I don't know, maybe Jesse and I even gave each other a hug, though I wouldn't let that get around. But I do know this—there were plenty of grins, smiles, and one or two thank-yous to God.

Chapter Thirty-Three

WRAPPING UP

J
E
N
N
I
F
E
R

Jesse and I sat outside the lab tent in the late afternoon sun. It felt good to be out of all that rain and mud and moving earth. It also felt pretty good to be alive.

"You don't remember anything?" Jesse asked.

"Nope. Just the water gushing out of the ground. And that when it comes to breathing water, I'm not such a good fish."

He nodded, but I could tell he wanted to hear more.

"What's up?" I asked.

"I don't know, it's just . . . remember how when we were going through the different dimensions, you kept going higher into the brighter light but I got stuck?"

"Yeah."

"And you said it was about the choices we made. You know, about God and Jesus and stuff?"

I nodded.

"Well, what exactly—"

"Hey! Get back here!"

We looked up just in time to see Maximilian run past, followed by, well by another Maximilian. Thanks to our little adventure there were now two of the cute fur balls. Running behind them was the last of the Animal Control workers from Jerusalem. They'd spent all day carting off the animals that had gathered around the staging area. Now they were down to one last worker, a super-grumpy old man, who was filling the last truckload. He'd already caught a couple crocodiles, some of the creepier desert snakes, and a dozen even creepier lizards. True, they weren't my favorite creatures, but he'd really handled them pretty rough and mean.

Now he was after two rather rambunctious chimpanzees.

But, first, he'd have to get around Hazel. "Leave them alone!" she shouted after him. "They're my pets!"

"Would love to, lady," he yelled back at her, "but the ignorant things got my keys."

"They are not ignorant!"

We had to grin as they all ran past us in one direction.

"Get back here you disgusting animals!"

"Sweeties!"

We grinned bigger as they ran past us the other direction.

"Sweeties!"

"Get back here you filthy primates!"

After they'd rounded the corner and were out of sight, I turned back to Jesse. I'd been thinking how to tell him about Jesus—you know, how I'd asked Him to forgive me of all my sins, and how even when I was a major loser, the Pure saw me as pure."

Unfortunately, we had another interruption.

"So," Jake said as he stepped out of the lab tent. "How are the two love birds?"

I felt my ears turning red. But Jesse, sensing my embarrassment and being the kind, thoughtful boy he is, changed subjects. Motioning to the lab tent, he asked Jake, "Any news on your priceless treasures?"

Earlier, a street beggar had talked Jake into buying a box full of "ancient and mysterious artifacts." Jake fell for the sales pitch and we'd been teasing him ever since.

"Yeah," I said. "Any news on that genuine moon rock?"

Jake motioned back to the tent. "Dad's running some tests now."

"Right," I said. "And how 'bout that wizard's wand?"

Jesse joined in. "Or that tooth from Bigfoot?"

"Come on guys," Jake said. "The dude promised it was all real."

I nodded. "And if you can't trust a street beggar, who can you trust?"

Before Jake could answer, Dad stepped out of the tent. "Well, son," he said, "you just might have something after all."

"I knew it!" Jake gave me a triumphant grin. "It's that coin from the lost continent of Atlantis, right?"

"Uh, no."

"That ray gun from the crashed UFO?"

"Sorry."

He wilted slightly.

"But we did find an interesting piece of iron spike."

"An iron spike?" Jake muttered. "Wonderful."

"It just might be," Dad said.

"What do you mean?"

It's the type of spike the Romans used to execute prisoners in the time of Christ."

"Like what they drove through their hands and feet?" Jake asked.

Dad nodded.

I sat up a little straighter. This definitely had my interest. "In Jesus' time?"

Jake knew exactly what was going through my head and asked, "Do you think . . . I mean, could it be?"

Dad shrugged. "Who knows. But for people to have passed it down over all these centuries, somebody must have thought it was valuable."

I traded looks with Jake. Was it possible?

"First thing tomorrow we'll put it into the Machine and see what comes up." Dad turned back toward the tent. "Nice work, son."

"Of course." Jake pretended to yawn. "What did you expect?"

Dad could only shake his head as he stepped inside.

"Better let me give you a hand with that," Jake said,

following him. "You know, in case you've overlooked something."

It was my turn to shake my head.

Once they were gone, Jesse asked. "Is that important? The spike, I mean?"

"It might be. Like Dad said, for people to keep it so long. Who knows, maybe it actually is one of the spikes they crucified Jesus with."

Jesse frowned. "You know, I never understood why that was so important. Jesus dying on the cross and all. It sounds pretty gross."

"Yeah, I'm sure it was. For God to punish Jesus for all the wrong we've ever done, it must have been real messy."

Jake quietly quoted, "The Pure making you pure."

I nodded.

"But . . . why you?"

I looked at him.

"I mean, no offense, but why did He choose to make you pure over the rest of us?"

"No," I shook my head. "He wants to make *everybody* pure . . . so we can *all* be with God in heaven."

"Everybody?"

I nodded. "But we have to let Him. We have to obey Him."

Jake got real quiet. "We're back to choices again, aren't we? Just like those people choosing to get onto the ark."

I nodded.

"But instead of the ark, it's . . ."

"Jesus," I said softly. "That's right. And it's a choice anybody can make." I hesitated, "Even you."

Once again he got quiet and thoughtful.

But it lasted only a second before we were interrupted by someone shouting from the staging area, "Help me! Please!"

We looked at each other then jumped from our chairs and ran toward the voice. I had no idea what to expect until we rounded the last tent and saw the two chimpanzees jumping up and down on the giant cage in the back of the Animal Control Truck. They were really

Ooo-ooo-ahh-ahh-eee-eee!
Ooo-ooo-ahh-ahh-eee-eee!

going at it.

Hazel was there, too. "Bad Maximilians! Bad Sweeties!"

She was not happy. And for good reason. Somehow the two chimps had locked the Animal Control guy inside the cage.

"Help me!"

And, for some reason, the grumpy old man wasn't nearly as grumpy. Terrified, yes. Grumpy, no. Being roommates with all those slithering snakes and creepy crawlies he'd been so mean to probably didn't help.

"Get me out of here!"

"Sweeties!" Hazel had crawled on the truck's hood and was climbing onto the roof where the chimps continued jumping up and down. "This is not funny!" But the sweeties seemed to disagree. And when she reached them, they started playing keep away with the keys, tossing them back and forth.

Meanwhile, the Animal Control man had pressed himself tightly against the bars, trying to avoid the creatures.

He really wasn't in trouble, but he was definitely freaked, which served him right.

Up on the roof, Hazel put one hand on her hip and held out the other demanding her furry friends give her the keys. They probably would have if Maximilian Number One (or was it Maximilian Number Two?) suddenly wondered what they would taste like. In one quick move he tilted back his head, opened his mouth and—

"NO SWEETIE!"

—dropped them inside.

Maximilian Number Two (or was it Number One?) thought this was the funniest thing he'd ever seen and started laughing and howling.

Maximilian Number One (or was it Number Two?) grinned back, then swallowed them, and—

"NOOO . . ."

BUUUURP-ed

to which both animals threw themselves down on the roof laughing, howling, and rolling back and forth.

"Help me!" the old man shouted. "Nice snakies, nice snakies!"

"Maximilians, no! Bad Maximilians!"

"Ooo-ooo-ahh-ahh-eee-eee."

"Ooo-ooo-ahh-ahh-eee-eee."

Try as we might, Jesse and I couldn't help but join in the laughter. Yes, there were plenty of important things to talk about. And, yes, there would probably be lots more dangers and adventures to face. But at least for now, at least for this minute, it was time to enjoy the:

"NICE SNAKIE, SNAKIES!"
"BAD SWEETIES!"
and, of course, all the

OOO-OOO-AHH-AHH-EEE-EEE
OOO-OOO-AHH-AHH-EEE-EEE-ing.

WHAT IF...

What if you could listen to actual conversations from the Bible? Dr. Mackenzie's brilliant and quirky group of young scientists have found a way to play them back using a machine that creates super-realistic holographs. Hang out with Noah and his floating zoo. Or, watch Jesus perform miracles.

Dr. Mackenzie is no stranger to crazy inventions. He has a lot of them. His twin kids Jake and Jen encounter several as they learn to love a dad they barely know. Their mom died, and now they live in Israel with Dr. Mackenzie. Together, they'll uncover powerful Biblical scenes while rediscovering their new lives as a family.

Available in print and digital editions everywhere books are sold.

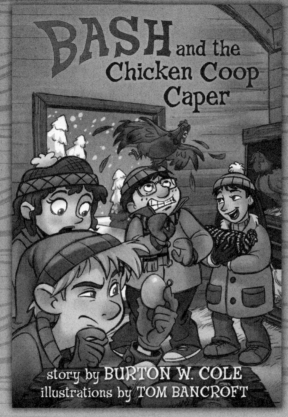

THERE'S A NEW GIRL IN TOWN...

Meet, Catie Conrad – a typical, tween, Christian girl with, oh, the weight of the world on her shoulders. And if it isn't bad enough that no one seems to understand the social pressures of being the greatest at everything, donning the latest fashions, and carrying the trendiest technology, Catie's dad is about to uproot her and her family to an Indian reservation during spring break for his job.

Coming to bookstores everywhere in Fall 2014!